Mosi-oa-Tunya

THE THUNDERING SMOKE

BOOK ONE
THE PRICE OF FREEDOM

GUY QUIGLEY

The Thundering Smoke
Book One: The Price Of Freedom
Copyright 2025 by Guy Quigley

ISBN 978-1-967421-16-9 (Paperback)
ISBN 978-1-967421-17-6 (Hardback)
ISBN 978-1-967421-15-2 (eBook)

Printed in the United States of America

This is a work of fiction. Names, characters, places, and incidents either are the product of the author's imagination or are used fictitiously. Any resemblance to actual events or locales or persons, living or dead, is entirely coincidental.

Published by ThunderSmoke Media LLC

DEDICATION

This book is dedicated to my wonderful wife Wendy, a true child of Africa, my soul mate, partner, mother of my children, and best friend for over fifty-four years.

ACKNOWLEDGEMENTS

To my parents, Joseph Quigley and Mother Josephine Quigley, the ultimate thespians. He was a violin virtuoso who was as comfortable playing the classics as he was an Irish jig. While she was an exceptional actress/director who could watch a film and later write the script from memory. These guiding lights taught me the art of self-expression. Without their love, knowledge, encouragement, and early guidance, this novel may never have been possible (RIP)

AND

To my mother-in-law, Stella Horton, a sophisticated lady and healer with significant hands-on knowledge about Africa and its wildlife. Also, thanks to my father-in-law George Horton, the finest hunter I have ever known with bush skills that were unquestionable. I savor those many nights spent around a roaring campfire while lions mated in the distance, hearing countless true stories stranger than fiction. And to the many collectively unknown who helped shape this story. (RIP)

AND

A very special thank you to my eldest daughter Claudine Quigley Piechotta, who embarked on the amazing and time-consuming challenge of editing and adapting this manuscript. With her input and prowess, she painlessly and graciously undertook the task of rewriting my manuscript. A very special and talented lady.

ABOUT THE AUTHOR

Guy Quigley was born in Ireland to a second-generation thespian family. He was educated in Ireland, where he left the theatre and entered the business world. He is married with three children and has six grandchildren. From 1970 through the early 80s, he built a 40,000-acre cattle ranch in Zambia, Africa, housing 5,000 heads of cattle and imported 100 pedigree Semmintaler cattle from Bavaria, Germany, via three Boeing 707 Skybarn aircraft, establishing the first pedigree Semmintaler stud in the south-central African country.

In his spare time, he wrote two fictional novels — one, a children's story, *The Little People*, and the other, a historical fiction saga, *The Smoke That Thunders*; now, after over forty years, it is being published as a trilogy.

In the United States, he successfully developed and marketed an award-winning cold remedy zinc lozenge under the franchise name COLD-EEZE,® establishing the US zinc-lozenge marketplace. To market the product, he formed The Quigley Corporation in 1989, which became a public entity on February 7, 1991, trading on the NASDAQ under the symbol (QGLY). His product COLD- EEZE® is available throughout the United States. He retired in 2009 and returned to his writing, which has been of tremendous therapeutic value and comes full circle to his birth roots. He has written three more books, *The Rebel Son with an* (Audio Book), *Hellevator*, and a soon-to-be-published cold-war spy thriller, *Predators at the Gates*, which will also be available as an audiobook. Along with his novels, he has written several award-winning movie scripts. In his film production endeavors, He is the ex-producer of *Magic Boys* (*Diamond Heist*) in the EU. He is also the ex-producer of the spoof *Breaking Wind* and the ex-producer of *Wicked Blood.* Utilizing his ThunderSmoke Media Company, he produced the 2015 award-winning movie *Apparition.* His latest film production from ThunderSmoke Media is *Impuratus,* a thriller suspense horror movie due for release in North America and worldwide distribution in October 2023.

www.guyquigley.com www.thundersmokefilms.com

PREFACE

For over a decade, along with my wife, I owned and operated a cattle ranch in the south-central African country of Zambia. Without TV and little reliable world news, we were somewhat cloistered and spent most evenings listening to true stories dating back to the last century. Coming from an Irish thespian background did not make me the ideal worker of the land, yet I learned the hard way by trial and error.

My motivation to write a book stemmed from the endless stories I learned. Hence, at every spare moment I had, I started to handwrite my story utilizing my knowledge of Ireland, her history, and Africa I came to know and love and attempted to weave them together in an action-adventure love story. After a couple of chapters, it all seemed to fall into place, and I could not wait to put more words on paper, albeit they were barely legible from my terrible art of scribbling.

So was born my story of a fictional character called Tom Sutton, who, during the Irish Liberation War of 1919, under the inspiration of Michael Collins the top Irish revolutionary leader of the time was overtly successful in his execution of disrupting British rule. Being a man with a price on his head, he loses his wife Grace - the love of his life - in a brutal rape executed by Black and Tans at a bloody raid on his home.

Believing his son Sean suffered the same deadly fate as Grace, he is forced to escape, and by sheer misunderstanding, he finds himself on the vast continent of Africa, sinking into the shame and degradation of alcohol. By a strange twist of fate, a little girl with a bowl of soup and the fear of the loss of her dying father brings him back from living death to the reality of the child's pain and future.

Together with the young girl Heidi and Weasel Byrne, his only friend from the troubled Irish times, they travel north through the small working goldmines of Southern Rhodesia to the north of Mosi-oa-Tunya (The Smoke That Thunders-Victoria Falls), finally settling in Northern Rhodesia. There, a new life of intrigue, crime, adventure, and love is born until his past comes back to haunt him.

My problem in writing a novel was the fact that it was hand-written and two-finger typed. There were no computers back in the mid-seventies, so errors abounded. It took over eighteen months to get my writing into some form of a legible manuscript. So, what did I learn from such an experience? Patience is definitely a virtue.

The story, in my mind, was chapters ahead of what was being handwritten. Several times, there was writer's block. That taught me to think hard and continue to write, even if nobody liked it. This book was my first attempt at writing, and since then, I have written three other books and several screenplays.

CONTENTS

CHAPTER 1

The Price of Freedom

Digging the trench of sacrifices even deeper for a greater cause is an ideology most freedom fighters live and die by. The fight for freedom always comes at a hefty cost, and the Irish War of Independence was no different. Long before the Great Depression drove the world into financial despair and ruin, a liberation movement emerged in Ireland some fifty years prior. Tired of heavy taxation, primarily caused by massive exports of raw materials, the Irish Catholic populace in the south no longer desired to live under British rule. They craved self-governance and emancipation from the Crown.

In 1886, British Prime Minister William Ewart Gladstone introduced the first Home Rule Bill to grant Ireland a measure of self-governance and national autonomy. It failed to pass, and its subsequent attempt in 1893 also failed.

It took another nineteen years, two generations of effort, empty negotiations, and violence-induced implementation to introduce a "free tomorrow" for the Third Home Rule Bill. It passed in 1912. In response to the bill, the Unionists in Ulster, the Protestant north of Ireland who desired to maintain a union with Britain, formed the Ulster Volunteer Army to prevent the domestic self-government of Ireland. A year later, the Irish in the south had formed the Irish Volunteer Army, mostly in response to the Ulster Volunteers, and Ireland became officially divided and poised for a civil war.

Thomas Edward Sutton was among the hundreds of young Irish men who had tasted the promise of freedom as part of the Irish Volunteer Army. In the early days, when he was courting Grace, he had been able to keep his persuasions and activities secret from the Gallaghers, his prospective in-laws. They did not condone the idea of the Irish civil war or any rebellion that would bring them to that brink.

Conversely, his bravery, rebelliousness, and charm had initially seduced Grace. She first met him on Grafton Street during a trip to Dublin with her parents in 1910. He was a confident, independent, and cocky twenty-year-old. His ardent blue eyes and winsome smirk entrapped her heart almost instantly. At that first meeting in the marketplace, he had promised to write to her, and surprisingly, he did, with letters full of defiance and passion. Written correspondence soon evolved into face-to-face meetings. Tom was a determined and ambitious young man, and most weekends, he would find some way to Enniskerry to see Grace, whose family lived near a lake close to the Wicklow mountains. He even attended mass sometimes just to get into her parent's good graces. Pleasantries across the church courtyard soon became stolen afternoons. She was keenly aware that her parents weren't fond of her new beau, so she learned to time her village errands with Tom's visits to avoid their disapproving commentary. Nothing could keep them from one another, and a year later, their hearts and minds had become inextricably bound.

As the violence intensified across the country, Grace could no longer keep Tom's activities or her feelings for him from the Gallaghers. Without her parents' blessing, Tom and Grace married in the Summer of 1912, just a few months after the third Home Rule Act passed. A year later, they welcomed their son Sean.

The Home Rule victory and the birth of their son were supposed to be the end of their struggles with Britain and with the Gallaghers. For a time, it worked. Grace's mother had become smitten with the baby like any Nana would. She had even begun to visit regularly, bringing her father along on at least two occasions when he was sure that Tom would not be home. Grace remained confident that she could mend the divide with her parents once the dust had settled, and she hoped that they might even come to see promise in Ireland's liberation. She was, after all, their only child. And she was certain that her beautiful raven-headed, green-eyed boy would aid in the reconciliation. If they could see what a loving husband and devoted father Tom was, she was sure that they would come to understand his passion for Ireland, too. Maybe they could even learn to accept him someday.

However, before the Act could be adopted, it was suspended due to the onset of the First World War. On September 20, 1914, with Home Rule within grasp, John Redmond MP, leader of the Irish Nationalist Party, pledged support to the Allied cause and urged his countrymen to enlist. Half of the enlisted Irish came from the South and half from the North. Many began to abandon the idea of a free Ireland, even those who had previously been in favor. But Tom, like many other young men, refused to enlist on principle and remained committed to the cause, even if it was only in his heart for the time being.

As Tom expected, through the tedium of war, support for the British war effort soon began to wane amongst young Irish Nationalists. Growing rage of betrayal within the nation led to another wave of mutiny against the British, as emerging forces like Sinn Fein (Irish Republican Party) gained strength and took up the cause, culminating in the Easter Rising, a bloody insurrection for Irish sovereignty in 1916.

Tom and his friend Timothy had joined the cause like so many young men, fighting directly under the authority of Michael Collins. The nation became enraged when the six-foot-three American Eamon De Valera, Commandant of Boland's Mill, was subsequently arrested and sentenced to death for his role in the insurrection. He would be later released due to rising political tensions and go on to become the leader of Sinn Fein. Opposition to Britain's handling of the uprising would eventually lead to a resurgence of Irish public opinion towards nationalism and Sinn Fein's victory in the election of 1918.

But any reparations that Tom and Grace might have made with her parents at the beginning of the war crumbled in the wake of the Easter Rising. When the Gallaghers could no longer ignore Tom's involvement in Sinn Fein and the violence that had been erupting across the country, they set their sights on America. They wanted Grace and Sean to come with them, but Grace could not leave. She loved Tom desperately, and she believed in his fight, even if her hope for victory was failing. She had no choice but to stand by her husband. For this stalwart loyalty to Tom, her parents had effectively disowned her. They left her their family cottage, for they had no other progeny and a promise of prayers for her redemption. With no further means of contact, Grace stood on the dock one misty summer morning in 1917, clutching Sean's little hand. Tears wet her face as she watched her parents turn away from the railing, taking a piece of her heart with them across the Atlantic.

Tom Sutton modelled himself after Mícheál Seán Ó Coileái or Michael Collins, as he was known to the British. A member of the Irish Republican Brotherhood, Collins was a soldier, a revolutionary, and an adept Irish politician. After participating in the Easter Rising and subsequent imprisonment, he rose to the ranks of the Irish Volunteers and Sinn Fein, becoming a leading figure in the struggle for Irish independence. Like Collins, Tom had become highly engaged in the rebellion after his involvement in the Easter Rising. His tactical efforts and strategic execution of multiple successful raids had made him instrumental in their efforts. He had risen the ranks and earned himself quite a pompous reputation for a twenty-seven-year-old.

Tom's idealism and passion drove his ambition, and his orphan childhood and subsequent scrappy youth had given him the grit and resilience required for the job. Tom idolized Michael Collins. After all, not every man could become both the Director of Intelligence of the Irish Republican Army and Commander-in-chief of the National Army. Similarly, Tom had always been a natural leader, and he liked to believe that at least his passion for the cause matched that of Michael Collins himself.

Clandestine raids and subversions provided little financial sustainability or rewards. But it was for a higher cause that Tom worked so tirelessly. So, the little family lived simply, and Tom never took his wife's loyalty for granted. He understood that she had given up so much for him and his ambitions. His activities had cost her parents and had deprived her of any luxuries she might have hoped for in her young married life. He recognized that she had justified to herself that his love was enough compensation, and he felt the weight of her sacrifice. He knew that this kind of life could not be forever.

Three years had passed since her parents had left. Three years of skirting the authorities and living on borrowed time. Even though Sean kept Grace occupied and sporadically injected their constant stress and anxiety with the levity and joy only a child can, Tom knew that he would have to extricate himself from this mission soon, or it would kill his wife's spirit. Besides, it was getting dangerous.

By the Autumn of 1920, as Tom's activities grew more nefarious, the family began living almost exclusively out of harm's way at the Gallagher family cottage. The little cottage that Grace's parents had left her, above Lough Tay Lake near the Wicklow mountains, was the only inheritance she had claimed from her estranged family. This humble but comfortable dwelling provided what the little family sought most in these turbulent times: some peace, far away from the dangers and uneasiness of Dublin. Here, Tom could abandon the stealth, the gunshots and grenades, and hasty raids at unholy hours. Adrenaline and fear were replaced here by an ancient serenity connecting him to the land and his past. The very air itself seemed to surround the Sutton family home with an invisible shield of protection.

The quaint, white-washed cottage had a thatched roof that had lovingly weathered to an earthy brown through countless showers of rain. It was nestled as the proud subject of a Campbell watercolor on a high slope skirted on each side by grassy plains. In recent months, the Black and Tans had begun to make their way out of the city and into the countryside, disturbing and destroying the tranquility of even these rural places. The wee2k before, villages in County Clare on the west coast and in County Meath, just north of Dublin, had been burned.

For the last two nights, Tom had had lucid nightmares of pooled blood on the little stone pathway outside their front door. Waking breathlessly, he would reach for his gun and creep to the window only to find the same pathway illuminated in the moonlight, unharmed and dotted with shamrock. Here, the frightful night sky of Dublin, cloaked with ominous grey clouds, was replaced with free, unadulterated starlight and a sky that stretched out from the majestic mountain range behind them to beyond the lake below. Grace and Sean often lay on a blanket, bundled up together, their eyes transfixed on the heavens above, naming all the stars.

But even the expansive sky in beautiful County Wicklow could betray them now, he thought. Tom could no longer escape the danger in his head. He knew what the Black and Tans were capable of, and none of them was safe anymore, anywhere.

Stepping outside, Tom breathed in the moist late September air and gazed out over the lake. Instead of the brassy city streetlights that often reflected horrific and unfortunate events, the gentle moonlight here shimmered over the gentle ripples on the lake below. The freedom Tom wanted for the city could almost be found here in moments like this, he thought. He allowed himself to relax and breathe in the liberation. How he longed for that same sense of freedom to encompass the entire nation, the way this remote cottage stood so resolutely and unencumbered. Since the Gallaghers' departure, this home had offered them refuge from the outside world and a chance to escape the chaos that was rippling through the country. The warmth and shelter the little cottage provided were priceless in this world that seemed so unstable. When he could quiet his mind, Tom felt connected to its ancient past. He felt grounded.

Tom and her little son Sean, her boys as she liked to call them, had left early that morning to collect chanterelles. Sean loved early morning adventures with his father. Before sunrise, they had set out to search for the mushrooms near the Beech Trees while the fog still clung to the grass and the birds were just beginning to wake. There had been a couple of warm days since the last rain, so the timing was perfect. While she waited for their return, Grace tidied up the little space, started a fire, and set the kettle on for tea. Despite their imperfections and dull hue, the cottage's uneven wooden floors bore the tread of at least four generations' worth of familiar footsteps. The well-used fireplace, now ablaze, took prominence at the far corner, harboring a black iron hook where Grace sadly recalled her mother hanging her Nana's cast iron kettle. That same kettle now hung from some unfamiliar fireplace in America. To its left, Tom's favorite armchair sat in anticipation, the Sunday Independent sprawled across the arm, displaying the latest atrocity in black and white. A faded brown wool rug lay underfoot, lovingly threadbare in spots. Sean would lay here at night, elbows down, chin in hands, listening to Tom's wild Irish tales of little people and fairies with wide eyes and curiosity.

Mammy's old rocker anchored the space, a bittersweet reminder of a happier time. On the far side of the small kitchen area stood a gas stove with an oven, a modern invention that her father had installed ten years before. An early twentieth-century continental floral couch sat proudly against the plaster wall framed on each side by windows facing East. This couch was Grace's mark on her home, something they had bought for the place from Dublin when they first took occupancy. A lace tablecloth adorned the square wooden kitchen table that had once been her sweet grandmother's. Grace sighed. The table was already set for breakfast, awaiting their return.

Upstairs, the bedroom loft where they all slept was small but cozy. Sean's small wooden trundle was pushed against the left wall. It was the same tiny bed Grace had slept on as a child. A lantern stood next to their bed, once her parents' bed, on a diminutive, wobbly side table. On a moonlit night, you could see the jacks, or outhouse, from the small loft window, which, although close, seemed like a half-mile walk in the early hours of a frigid Irish winter morning. But Grace didn't mind. Now all this was hers. Now it was her new kettle and not Nana's that stood at the ready. She didn't mind pumping her water, for the lake had an endless supply. She had always dreamed that they would modernize the place and bring it into the twentieth century. Maybe even build on to it. But that dream had faded over the last year. One thing was for sure: this place was her home, and she would never exchange it for that cold, dingy terrace safe house in Dublin and the chaos of a world she didn't want to know.

Through the window, she observed the rhythmic calmness radiating from the ripples on the surface of the lake. After a heady week of secret planning or another seemingly endless night of life and death encounters, she would often find Tom standing on the edge of the lake, staring into the calming water. Today, the wind danced freely around the cottage, rustling the thatch playfully. This was a good day, Grace decided.

Tom was not the only one living in distress. Nearly every day, a constant fear nagged at the back of her mind. No matter how busy she kept herself with Sean and the daily chores, it was always there. While Tom was off at night battling for his freedom cause, she lay in bed visualizing images of stray bullets that could shatter her husband's skull or pierce his heart. These invasive thoughts could drain the blood from her face in an instant, any time of day, no matter what she was doing. If Tom was not supposed to come home on a certain night and there was a knock at the door, her fingertips would go cold against the doorknob in anticipation. Would she find a messenger with a chilling missive, tasked to convey the death of her husband, or just a friendly neighbor with a basket of cheese or eggs and a ruddy grin?

While these morbid thoughts constantly plagued her mind, Grace was unperturbed and happy today. Today, her husband and son were safe inside their little haven, without a care in the world. She unlatched the upper half of the door and stuck her head out to soak in this beautiful day. A sudden breeze whipped up, causing her long auburn hair to unravel and whip around her face, grazing her sea-green eyes.

She was a classic Irish beauty with pale milky skin and just a lot of freckles on her nose and cheeks. It was no secret that she had captured the eye of many of the eligible young men from the village. Many whom her parents would have more readily approved of. But it was Tom who had snatched up her heart and held it still. Her loveliness wasn't merely skin deep. Grace was passionate and loving to a fault. She was the kind of person who always put others first and never let anyone feel left out. It was, in fact, that kindness and conviction that had ensnared Tom Sutton, who, being an orphan, had never known such love and support in his life.

Laughing, Grace kicked the bottom half of the door open with a nudge of her foot while she grasped her long red hair with both hands. Her eyes searched for what was hers. Scanning the lush green hills beyond the lake, she spied two figures in the distance. They had returned from their quest, baskets in hand brimming with mushrooms. Sean looked just like her, save for her red hair, but his mannerisms were patently Tom's. His thick black, wavy hair tossed about in the breeze as he tried to match the man's gait beside him, running in between steps to catch up. She watched as they stopped at the edge of the lake to skim flat stones, disrupting the smooth surface with ripples as the rocks tripped rhythmically in threes and fours. She could faintly hear Sean giggle and chatter in the distance.

If only this moment could be frozen in time, she thought. But days like this always came to an end. Tonight, Tom would go back to a battle that Grace was starting to believe was futile. And she would return to her nervous solitude. Life was as robust and fragile as glass, clear and impenetrable, yet so easily shattered in an instant without warning. But she quickly dismissed these unwanted thoughts. Days like this one were a blessing that none of the Suttons took for granted.

Grace had been so caught up in her thoughts that she had failed to see Sean making a dash up the hill toward her. They had spied her watching them from the cottage door.

"I'll only give you a 20-yard head start this time, Sean," Tom shouted from behind.

The boy didn't turn around but kept up his charge. This was serious business. "Alright, Da. The first one to Mammy wins."

"Don't forget the mushrooms," Grace implored, calling out to them.

Tom patiently waited for his son to cover half the distance while he scooped up their baskets. He didn't want to ruin the little boy's expectations of a win. His comparatively enormous steps covered the rising hill swiftly, but seeing Sean's pace slow from exhaustion, he quickly feigned a cramp. That was all Sean needed. Seeing his father pause, he pushed forward. He had his father's competitive nature, and Tom loved that about him. Tom wanted him to believe in himself, trust his instincts, and not put limitations in his way. More importantly, he always wanted him to feel supported, not the way he had felt growing up as an orphan.

As the father and son neared the cottage, Grace cheered them on, holding out her arms in a warm invitation to the little boy. His mother's enthusiasm only spurned him forward with a new wave of energy as his father ran comically slowly behind. Sean leapt forward to cover the last bit of slope before hitting the flat ground connecting the path to the cottage. He landed in his mother's arms with the widest grin wrapped around his cherub face. The little runner's ruddy-windswept face was kissable, and Grace scooped him into her arms as Tom fell at her feet gasping dramatically and laughing, mushrooms spilling from the baskets he had dropped.

The little boy announced his victory to his parents, "I won, I won, I won!"

"Your boy has the speed of a racehorse, Mrs. Sutton." Tom winked at his wife as he picked up the chanterelles with a grin.

"I bet he has the appetite of a horse too. Come on, you two, the tea is freshly brewed. I also have a lemon pudding cake and some warm scones just out of the oven. How many pieces of the lemon pudding will you finish off today, my big growing boy?" Grace jested, tussling Sean's hair lovingly.

The mention of the cake made the little boy jump up and down ecstatically, "Lemon pudding? Is there lemon syrup drizzle, too?"

Grace gave him a peck on the cheek and patted him on the bottom. "Yes, my child. Now go off quickly and wash up while I take the kettle off." And with that, she turned inside.

The aroma of the tea and delicacies made their stomachs rumble, and after a hasty wash-up at the sink pump, Tom and Sean flopped down on the couch. Tea was served in her parent's best blue china, too delicate to travel to America, and perhaps, in some small way, Grace imagined that it had been intended as a gift to the only daughter a mother may never see again.

Grace poured the tea as Tom and Sean pulled themselves to the table and ravenously helped themselves to the pudding cake and scones that were piled onto a three-tier white china serving stand, another Gallagher treasure. After Sean had filled his plate to the brim, Grace placed the blue china cup with its designated saucer on the table before he and Tom drizzled the lemon syrup on all their servings. A subtle autumn breeze wafted into their cottage through the half-open window and gently caressed the pastel blue curtains, spreading the aroma of tea, sweet treats, and laughter into every corner. "This is what home should be," thought Grace.

The family chatted, with Tom and Sean arguing about whose rock skimmed the farthest over the lake and Grace laughing at their childish banter.

"Mammy, Da was cheating. My rocks skimmed the lake five times, and his were drowned after only two skips!" Sean protested with his mouth full.

Holding his right hand to his heart in a dramatic manner, Tom feigned injury. "Boy, are you accusing your father of making up lies?"

The boy furiously shook his head left and right while his parents tried not to laugh at their guileless young boy.

"How many times have I told you not to speak with your mouth full? And Tom, if Sean says your rock drowned, then it must have." Grace said with finality as she gave her son a pat on the head and winked at Tom.

Seeing the mother and son team up against him warmed Tom's heart. He wondered what good he had done in his life to have deserved such a family. Observing her husband quietly watching them with a faraway look, Grace assumed he was thinking of returning to the city.

The couple held each other's gaze in silence, both trying to comprehend what the future held for them without ruining the moment.

After breakfast, they played outside with Sean, soaking in the unusually sunny September day. For a while, Dublin was a distant thought. After a hearty supper of lamb stew and fresh chanterelles, Tom retired to his favorite armchair as Sean assumed his position by the fireplace for the next chapter of Peter Pan, his latest favorite. Grace joined them later and relaxed in the rocker with some knitting, listening to the latest battle between Captain Hook and Peter with childlike interest. It was perfect.

By the time they had cleaned up their tea, the sun had disappeared, and the cheery day had succumbed to nightfall. The panic and nervousness returned as the clock ticked each terrible second closer to 8 o'clock. Grace allowed the father and son a few more precious moments before they would be forced apart again. She looked adoringly at Sean playing on the rug with his trains as she picked up the dirty cups and plates and brought them to the kitchen sink. The empty glass milk bottle on the windowsill mocked her as it reflected the moonlight seeping through it. Nature was not her ally tonight.

Methodically, she stood by her cast iron sink and washed the dishes one at a time. Her mind worked on its own accord, and the horrid visions again consumed her thoughts. A cup slipped through her fingers. In an instant, one of her treasures lay by her feet, the corner of the cup painfully chipped with a crack running along one side. With adrenaline permanently piqued, the sound startled Tom, and he rushed to the sink. Seeing the fallen cup, he quickly picked it up and placed it carefully on the table. He took her trembling hands in his and interlocked her slender, soft fingers with his calloused ones. Despite the difference in size, their hands seemed to fit together perfectly. Sean looked up obliviously from his toys, smiled, and then went back to pulling his train over the bumpy rug, blissfully unaware of the tension that pulsed through his parents.

Tom slowly rubbed his thumb in circles on the back of Grace's hand, and when she still did not look up to meet his questioning gaze, he placed his finger under her chin and tilted her face to him.

Her porcelain skin was devoid of its usual pink hue, and her sensitive sea-green eyes watered at the corners, where dark circles of worry framed them. She smiled for Tom's benefit, locking him out of her state of mind. But the worry etched in her eyes betrayed her. This was not the first-time morbid thoughts had threatened to shatter their peace, and it wouldn't be the last. Tom pulled his wife to his chest and rested his hands loosely on her back.

"My love, why do you do this to yourself?"

Grace remained silent. She did not want Sean to hear their conversation. The two of them had never talked to their boy about what Tom did or where he disappeared for weeks at a time, although she was sure he had already heard too much.

She whispered, "I am fine. I just got lost for a bit. Go back to Sean; Murphy will be coming at any time. I'm almost finished." Tom looked for reassurance, and when she gave him the slightest nod coupled with a distant smile, he understood and joined Sean, dropping onto the rug beside him and his trains. Grace even joined them, and they spent the last of their precious time playing with their little boy, losing themselves in make-believe.

Murphy was Tom's commander and a trusted friend for the purposes of their endeavors at least. He could be gruff sometimes, but he generally meant well. His automobile was the family's only reliable mode of transportation to Dublin these days. As expected, he pulled up outside their cottage at 8 pm sharp, a sight to see in these parts where automobiles were few and far between. Deftly and stealthily, the little family vacated their little home, not that there was any neighbor closer than a half mile away. This was not the first time they had made this journey at night. Grace hated going into the city, but she hated being alone even more. It had become too risky to leave her and Sean alone in the country alone, especially with the recent burnings. Even though Dublin was dangerous, there were pockets of allies across the city. There was protection and places where they could hide. Grace bundled up a sleepy Sean while Tom locked up the cottage. Murphy looked on silently, as he had done so often before, leaning against the car and smoking a cigarette. Tom approached him, whispered a few words, and took a quick drag of his cigarette. The driver got inside the car. After Tom had secured their luggage and helped Grace and his sleeping boy into the backseat, he claimed the passenger seat. The engine chugged, and with a low purr, they were off.

The drive to Dublin was eerily quiet. The night sky covered the world below with a thick blanket. Grace could make out Sean's breathing pattern by watching the movement of the child's chest rising and falling in the dim moonlight. The two men in the front were engrossed in cross whispers. She could never decipher their conversations and didn't want to know all the details. She had learned early on not to ask questions for all their sakes.

It was a long drive to Dublin, plenty of time for Grace's scattered thoughts to simmer up all sorts of fears. As her mind drifted from the mumbled conversation in front of her, she leaned her head against the side door panel. She kept her right hand on Sean's chest's warm, rhythmical movement as her sleeping boy dreamed deeply on her lap. The car progressed from serene, moonlit rolling hills of uninhibited green to portentous, grey buildings that harbored secrets she wasn't privy to. Desolate country roads that seemed oddly comforting to her began to funnel into a web of city streets and thoroughfares with cemented pavements and metallic lampposts, whilst their guiding moonlight became subservient in their presence. As the car passed by the tramways, Grace wondered if Sean would ever have a normal life. As much as she loved Tom, she did not want Sean to hide away from the world like this, sneaking around in the shadows.

If Tom had not been a wanted man, the Sutton family could have saved Murphy the nearly four-hour round-trip car ride by taking the steam tramway from Glendalough and then on to Dublin. But the journey from Lough Tay to Glendalough alone was already a twelve-mile pony & trap ride from their cottage, and since their month-long sojourns at the cottage had now been curtailed to weekend getaways, the journey by cart and tram had not only become dangerous but logistically impossible.

In recent weeks, British forces regularly travelled the tramway from Dublin to the counties and villages actively looking for Tom. The recent village burnings offered further evidence that the Black and Tans were no longer contained to the Dublin city limits. Grace wondered how this could all possibly lead to freedom now if they couldn't even be seen in public as a family. Where was their freedom? Was the sacrifice worth relinquishing Tom's seat at the table for birthdays, church on Sundays, and even Christmas? A tear rolled down her cheek, but before it could land on Sean's forehead and disrupt his sleep, she wiped it away angrily with the back of her left hand.

As the car turned towards Palmerstown, the streetlights were reflected in her despondent, glistening eyes as she stared blankly at the approaching city. Since it was well after 10 p.m. now, there weren't any passersby. It was almost peaceful outside, quiet and sleepy but definitely not serene. No one could be trusted these days, so Murphy drove them to the end of the street before stopping. Even though Murphy was essentially his superior, the one who doled out his orders from the top and compensated him, he was also his biggest fan. He knew of Tom's humble beginnings, and he believed that Tom had the making of a great leader. He had done what he could to keep him engaged in the effort all these years. And if that meant playing chauffeur to ensure his safety and that of his young family, that was a sacrifice he was willing to make. Loyalties aside, even this alliance had limitations here in Dublin. Thomas Edward Sutton's deteriorating relationship with the government forced Murphy to fear for his well-being and anonymity. So, he left them discreetly ten houses away and motored off before anyone could take note of his Model T stopping in the quiet of the night.

This abode had none of the charms of their Lough Tay cottage. Identical to all the other houses on the street, it was a small, nondescript brick terrace house with a slate roof. It stood sandwiched between its neighbors, determined to remain anonymous and unacknowledged. Stealing into the house quietly, Grace, Tom, and Sean, lifeless over his father's shoulder, quickly shut the door and bolted it before any prying eyes could seek them out. While Tom gently laid

Sean down in the smaller back room, Grace drew the thick maroon curtains shut in the front of the house, stifling even the penetrating streetlamp outside. Unlike their emancipated cottage home, where breathing was easy and predictable, this place was claustrophobic and devoid of emotional warmth. Instead of a cheerful floral couch, a second-hand brown corduroy sofa occupied the tiny space. Two cheap characterless wooden tables flanked it on both sides. The galley kitchen only held the most basic supplies and none of Grace's treasures. This was a transient place.

A black metal stand was tucked in the corner, laden with several days' worth of newspapers from "The Irish Times" and the "Irish Independent" to keep them abreast of the latest atrocities. It was merely a house for hiding, a place to lay low until the dust settled, a safe house. Grace made her way towards Sean's room, situated to the right of the main entrance, behind theirs, and stopped in the doorway. The utilitarian muslin blinds were pulled. A single gas table lamp illuminated the child's room as it flickered on the bare side table. The metal framed bed provided nothing more than a place to sleep. It was an adult-sized bed and had come with the house, as had theirs. Grace had often wondered what this room could be like if this was her real "home," decorated with new paneled curtains appliqued in lace, with a proper modern boy's bed covered with a bedspread in bright geometric patterns and colors that were now all the rage. But this wasn't home…it would never be home!

She watched Tom pull the thick bedspread over the sleeping boy's body and kiss him good night, repeating what he always said to the boy. "Sweet dreams, my brave little soldier. Know that I love you and Mommy the most. Your mother will always be my guiding light, and you, son, will be my anchor."

Crouching next to the bed, Tom placed feather-like kisses on Sean's forehead and eyes before dialing down the lamp. He stopped briefly to see Grace leaning against the doorframe, but he said nothing.

He knew where any conversation would lead. These conversations frustrated him, and he was too tired to argue. He wanted to box up his "cottage" contentment and take it to bed with him. He did not want to lose it to resentment. Why couldn't he just relish this moment while it lasted? The couple converged in their front bedroom and dressed for bed in silence, tension as thick as treacle. Tom settled back against the black metal frame bed, propped his head on the pillow, and lit a cigarette. The smoldering orange tip was the only source of light in the dark room.

Grace slid silently into bed, letting out all her emotions in one eructation. Everything she had been harboring throughout the day poured out in a plea for normalcy and peace, culminating in tears of desperation. As irritated as Tom felt unable to placate all sides, he was well aware of her concerns. When she had no more words to hurl at him, he gently pulled his wife to him. She, too, felt vulnerable and was quick to reciprocate the gesture, burying her face into his chest between intermittent sobs.

"When will this end? How long will I have to endure this, Thomas? For Sean's sake, please." Grace muttered longingly. Putting his cigarette out in the ashtray, he tried to comfort her through the tears that now wet his chest, "Soon darling...soon?"

Furiously, Grace sputtered, "The soon that never comes? Your irrational excuses for the cause are killing us. And Sean...he's growing up without you most of the time. He will grow up fatherless... don't you care?"

Tom stroked her hair, and she softened in his embrace. "Grace, don't cry, shh, please, my Macushla. You are my everything, and so is Sean. I'm here right now with you. And my love, you know it is not a foolish cause. You know why I do what I do. Please let it be for now. We had such a good day."

Defeated, Grace replied, "Tell me how, Tom? How can I not worry? I am scared all the time when you are gone – every waking moment! Every time you are out there - every time you come home a bit late."

With deeper resolve now, Grace sat up in bed, releasing herself from him. "How long am I to make excuses to Sean each time he wants to know when you're coming home? Or how shall I explain why we can't stay at the cottage anymore for fear that someone will find us." How do you expect me to go on like this, Tom, and for how long? We don't even know which of our neighbors we can trust. Is this your definition of freedom, Thomas? Do you know that I fear drawing the curtains apart or lighting the house? We can't have simple holiday outings like other normal families. I have endured it until now, for your sake…for Ireland's sake. But now, with the violence spreading and Sean growing up and asking more and more questions…you have so many enemies, Tom. They are always out there looking for you. But I need you, Tom. Your boy needs you. I need you to stop…please just stop!"

As Grace's resolve devolved into heaving sobs, Tom held her closer to his chest. This was not the first time she had been inconsolable, but it was by far the worst. He knew that they were in danger, and perhaps the time had come to give her a promise he intended to keep. He also feared that he was dangerously close to being either apprehended or killed, although he would never admit that to her. Maybe she was right; he had given all he could to the cause, and it was time for him to think of their future. They didn't deserve to be abandoned.

"This will all end soon, Macushla. I promise you, ok?" "When? No empty promises?" she said with conviction. "I promise, my darling, before this year is out. We will take Sean and move to America."

Tom kissed his wife deeply on her dry, trusting lips and pushed back the wet strands of hair from her cheeks. Her tears slowly subsided, and they nestled into their pillows and pulled the eiderdown up to their necks, the only real luxury they had in this dismal place. Tom wrapped Grace into him, limbs entwined in limbs. They got lost in each other, and their lovemaking cemented a promise for their future. As they lay naked in the darkness, wrapped in the warmth of each other's arms, he stroked his hair. He watched her eyelids become heavy, and she soon fell asleep. This beautiful, trusting angel of his had given up so much to love him all these years. It was time for him to put his family before his country.

CHAPTER 2

Dreaming of America

The dark sky over the brewery was mostly clear, save for a few lingering clouds sprawled across it. The rain had stopped only an hour or so before, but the misty chill still hung in the air. Puddles pooled on the uneven cobblestoned road, and nearby, a huddle of like-minded men, his compatriots, stood waiting. Wafts of cigarette smoke rose and diffused into the creeping fog. An adolescent, no more than seventeen, murmured under his breath and shuffled his feet restlessly.

Tom smiled at his nervousness - he had seen him around. But he wasn't happy that Murphy had sent this boy tonight on a man's mission. This night marked the end of an era for Tom, and he didn't need a tag-along if things went array. He had a built-in comfort level with his men. A level of comfort that had taken years to foster. They were all veterans and, ultimately, friends.

But it had been a year since he had promised Grace that they would leave, and dutifully, he had spent the last week making all the necessary arrangements for their departure. As the missions had become riskier and sometimes even reckless in recent months, Tom and his accomplices had had several near-death encounters. He had also garnished a position at the top of Britain's notorious most wanted list, which had forced him to keep away from his family for long jaunts of time when he had to remain in hiding. Their cottage had been abandoned, and Grace and Sean had been shuffled between Palmerstown and a network of other safe houses since the summer. Tom knew it could only get worse from here.

It was time their daily nightmares were replaced with restful, unadulterated sleep and hope for a real future, a future where Sean could grow up safely. It was no longer just the rational choice but the necessary choice. Maybe someday, when Ireland was finally free, they could return to their little cottage in Lough Tay, Tom hoped.

For a long time, Tom had compartmentalized his family's needs for his ideals. He had laid his allegiance at the feet of Ireland for the better part of his youth and early adulthood, and no one could say that he hadn't done all he could to advance the cause. Now, he feared he'd soon end up dead and leave Grace and Sean untethered, disillusioned, and destitute. It was time for someone else to pick up the mantle; his tour was over. He looked at the young recruit and wondered if it might be him.

He had to shake these looming thoughts. He was still a freedom fighter for Ireland tonight. As his hubris swelled, he looked to the stars and promised the night sky that tonight he would leave an imprint of undeterred resistance for the history books. He glanced over his shoulder at his boyos. When he was gone, the fate of his motherland would be left in their hands. Were they ready?

Under the looming brewery, Tom squinted at his watch. The hands were hard to decipher in the inky darkness. His heart quickened a little. Eleven-Fifteen. "Time to get into formation." Tom mused to himself before turning to roll out orders for his friends.

From his vantage point, he observed his accomplices. The frieze was quite humorous, given the seriousness of their mission. Not only were these grown men huddled together to keep warm, but they all had their hands shoved deep into the pockets of their black, knee-length trench coats and their mouths muzzled in their scarves. They looked oddly uniform like their outfits had been coordinated for the occasion. Upon Tom's summons, they all shuffled under the shadow of the brewery with their flat caps pulled down low over their faces to mask their identities. The young one nervously shifted his eyes from

Tom to the gang, sheepishly shoving his curly strawberry-blond hair under his dirty blue cap to fit in. It was obvious this was his first real ambush.

"Let's go through Murphy's plan one more time to make sure we are all clear, lads." Tom's voice was low but firm.

"Are you nervous, Tom? Is there something you're not telling us?" Joseph McCarthy asked, his small grey eyes peering out over his neck scarf. He was older than Tom by at least a decade, and despite his formidable, bulky stature, he seemed oddly as anxious as the rest.

"It had better or else." came Tom's answer to shore any doubts in the group.

The youngster looked down at his feet to avoid Tom's gaze. "For Christ's sake…the weather is… friggin' cold. I might… turn into a… snowman if I stay here for a… moment more," Weasel Byrne complained jovially, breaking any tension that still clung in the air.

Weasel, or Timothy Byrne as he was properly known, was smaller than Tom by several inches, with a wiry build. He had curly dark brown hair, deep-set blue eyes, a stubbly chin, and a cheeky face. He had been friends with Tom since they were boys. His family was from Killarney, and he had grown up near the orphanage where Tom had been committed. Together with his brother Shamus, they had been an inseparable trio in their teens, and the Byrne brothers had witnessed Tom and Grace's love story firsthand. He could always be relied on for comic relief, no matter how dire the situation was, and he had a reputation for speed. He had also eluded the authorities for years and was unofficially known as the "fastest man in Ireland."

"I'm telling you, boyos. I object to the idea of working next to the best stout in the world. What if something goes wrong? Then what, eh? We will end up blowing up the bloody brewery, and then where will I get me, stout lads?" They all cracked a smile under their scarves.

Shamus was Weasel's older brother and his notorious drinking partner. Taller and wider than Weasel, he had the same mane of unruly hair, but his face was softer, and his chin less chiseled than his brother's. Their love for stout and a good whisky were their trademark, and their reputations preceded them in Dublin.

"We ought to be very cautious, Thomas." mused Shamus. "I don't want milady to be blown up. The slightest spark could send her sky high. We don't want that now, do we, brother?"

"Damn right you are, Shamus. My life would be bleak without it." laughed Weasel.

"We don't want to deprive ourselves of some bitter yeasty goodness for a month of Sundays." continued Shamus, putting on a show now for their compatriots.

Even John Flynn, the fourth veteran, cracked a smile at this. He was a lanky chap with roaring red hair and a slight limp on his left leg, an injury likely incurred during one of these ambushes. He was the most serious in the group and tended to be sullen. He'd been a part of this racket longer than all of them and was keenly aware of the implications of their actions.

Shamus continued semi-seriously, "No, sir. If she goes up, my life's just not worth living, lads. What's life without a hangover." Young Patrick chuckled nervously.

Tom reprimanded the brothers, bringing them back to the task at hand, "Enough with the antics, you jesters. If we don't make it to the other side of this mission, there won't be any potcheen or stout at all for you two to get totally banjaxed."

Tom ushered them towards the middle of the road, and the five men followed. They gathered under a lamppost. McCarthy, Flynn, Shamus, and Weasel, together with their planner Murphy, had been working with Tom for over five years. They respected him, his concrete resolve and his loyalty to his country. It was compassion for the cause that had initially united them, but it was their friendship and competence as a team that had bound them to each other. They had become a force to be reckoned with, known in circles as the strongest unofficial junta against the British Black and Tans.

"If you take a look, you will notice there are six horse carts owned by the brewery, aligned on both sides of the road," Tom explained in half voice as the group huddled together.

"We did take that into consideration. Maybe, they don't want them inside at half past eleven on a Saturday night." Cracked Seamus. His sarcasm earned him an eye roll from Tom.

"The watchman leaves them out here every night, and so the Tans are accustomed to their presence. Every night, the horse carts are in the same spots, and every night the Tans drive down the middle of the road between them. Completely familiar. Now shift your focus to the manholes. They are each fifty feet apart, running flat against the road. They are also familiar. The Tans will drive right over these in their precious army lorries, thinking nothing of it, like they always do." Opening his coat, Tom revealed two round folded black painted cardboard discs.

"What are those, Tom?" Weasel asked

"Aye, let me see those," Shamus asked curiously, reaching for one, unfolding it and running his fingers over the edges.

"You'll notice, lad, that they match the real ones, but they're weightless. If we are going to hide down there for the ambush, we can't be fracturing our arms trying to lift them, now, can we? And besides, there goes any element of surprise." Tom said, showing the other to the boy as the men passed the disc around. Patrick nodded with understanding. Maybe this boy was going to be alright, Tom thought.

"Besides, it's not even McCarthy's weightlifting night." Weasel slammed back as the men chuckled at McCarthy's expense.

"So, we will simply hold the fakes over the holes until the lorries are above us. When I count four and give the signal, we'll go up. I'll discard my grenade under number four, and McCarthy, you'll throw yours under number one simultaneously."

"Hell's bells, why me, Tommy? Did I do something to piss you off, boyo?" McCarthy asked.

"Do you really want an answer for that, Joseph?" Tom said, lifting his eyebrow in half jest.

"Number one- you've got the best throw here. And, more importantly, you're already an expert at handling Stielhandgranates."

"Bejesus a potato masher?" piped up Patrick.

Tom threw a glance at the youth. "Right, you are, lad! In case the rest of you don't know, they are German *grenades that* detonate in under five seconds. A shit load of Germans blew themselves up mishandling these sticks in the war. So, I say, Joseph, you're the best man to handle it. And I'm going to be right by your side to count you in."

"Bloody hell, sounds insane to me," Weasel shrugged at the disclosure of the plan, "but if it turns the first and last truck into ashes, we'll be looking at possible forty dead Tans and a fecking inferno."

"Damn right Weasel and four wrecked armored lorries. Now, you all know I wouldn't be in favor of this kind of ambush if this was the British army. But it's not… these bastards are the Black and Tans, and we all know what they've done to our countrymen and to our women."

"The British recruit them from their jails, you know," added Weasel, whispering to Patrick. "They're a bunch of thugs and criminals. And then they do their dirty work for them."

"Alright, alright, Shamus and Flynn, you'll climb down the wall ladders to the Liffey. The river's low at that point, so you'll be roughly 10 feet away from the scene when the fireworks happen. Weasel, you're on the other side of the brewery in the alley." Their heads bobbed in affirmation.

"So, what do I do?" interrupted Patrick O'Leary, courage and fear beating together in his chest.

Tom did not wish to be held liable for this youth in such a critical situation. He had only ever worked with self-reliant grown men, fully capable of ensuring their own welfare, and he preferred it that way.

"You observe, lad," said Tom stoically. "You observe, you watch for interference, and you stay out of sight. I have no desire to witness your death or capture tonight. Understand?" Patrick was disappointed but too scared to confront any of his elders.

"Murphy's going to hear about this," said Tom, mumbling under his breath as he walked off to have a cigarette with Weasel. "Landing me with a boy, for Christ's sake. As if I'm not under enough stress with you two alcoholics, Flynn's wisecracks, and Joe McCarthy's big bumbling feet. Now I have to deal with a gossoon too!"

Patrick had overheard and approached them gingerly. "Sir, I'm more capable than you think. I shot two Tans in my first ambush at Crumlin a few weeks ago. But I went a little off on me second one. Couldn't hold meself back because me blood was pumping fast and all, and I shot the eejit in the arse."

The crew, who had been earwigging the conversation, erupted in laughter, piercing the still of the night. Tom shushed them but could not stop the corners of his mouth from twitching. He was used to maintaining a level of seriousness and had mastered the art of keeping his emotions in check. But this comic relief was good for the crew, especially tonight, so Tom decided not to bring down Patrick's youthful spirit.

"Alright, you smart-arsed gossoon, you go with Weasel. And for the love of this brewery, Weasel, please take care of the lad."

"Aye, captain," said Weasel with a grin, throwing his arm around the boy.

"Are we all set then, lads?"

Everyone shook their heads in the affirmative. They stretched out their limbs, re-buttoned their coats, and adjusted their scarves closer. It was not freezing, but the damp fog that now gathered around their feet sent chills up and down their spines.

"Gentlemen stay put until both lorries blow. I don't want any of you getting caught in the fray." Tom said as he rubbed his palms together to warm them.

"Alright, lads, Let's go.

"You heard the boss," said Weasel, his voice muffled by the scarf.

The three men and the youth scurried off in opposite directions while Tom and McCarthy made their way into the street. McCarthy struggled at first to lift the manholes, but he was exceptionally strong, and with a little bit of wrangling, he got them out, and Tom helped him carry them to the edge of the brewery wall. Then, they lowered themselves into the holes. Tom kept his head out and watched as McCarthy carefully placed the cutout over his open hole and descended. From a distance, the cover was indistinguishable and blended perfectly. Tom was satisfied. He did a final sweep of the entire scene before placing his cover above him and lowering himself down the cast iron steps into the sewer below.

McCarthy was obviously not the group's brains, but Tom could not ask for a better partner in these ambushes. He was very strong and always calm and methodical, perfect for this kind of work. But tonight, something was off.

"You are sure this will work?" McCarthy asked with unusual doubt in his voice as he met Tom somewhere in between the two manholes, being careful to watch where his large shoes landed in the muck underfoot.

Tom's mind was consumed with thoughts of this last ambush and the unwritten future that lay ahead of him. He exhaled and unclenched his sweaty fist, which he suddenly realized had been curled for some time. He rounded on the man defensively.

"It has to. We don't have another way, Joe. You know what your problem is? You worry too much. Now stop thinking, or you'll be off your game. We have the element of surprise, and that's our best weapon! There is no problem with Murphy's plan. Keep your brain coaxing maidens into bed and lying in the confession box to your parish priest, will ya." And he slapped the man on the shoulder.

McCarthy sensed that Tom was distracted. They'd been in this game too long together to not sense when something was off. But he took Tom's criticism and skillfully masked his response, throwing him a sly half smile as they leaned against the ladder at manhole number two. But there was a shift in the air, and it was not the diabolical stench underfoot. Tom was suddenly aware that it was his distracted mind that was the root of this tension, not McCarthy. He had to snap out of it. The dank air churning around them was beginning to suffocate him.

"So… this will be the last one." Tom softened. "Morbid bastard, aren't you?" McCarthy snorted.

"No, I mean it, Joe. Tonight's my last one. They have at least a mile-long record of my activities, and I can't always be such a lucky bastard, can I? So, I'm taking Grace and my boy, and we are leaving for America."

"I thought that might be it."

"So, it's got to be good tonight. Send me out with a bang...eh boyo."

"I've got your back, Sutton, as always. Do you think you'll be back?"

"Someday maybe...when there is a free Ireland. Grace and I will still own those twenty acres by Lough Tay. Hey, I might resort to farming or fishing all day long in the lake."

McCarthy laughed at the image of Tom as a farmer or a fisherman.

"Well, that's not likely. Lads and I will miss ya."

"I'll miss you too, Joe. I'll miss you all. You're like family." "Ah, don't get soft on me now, Sutton," said McCarthy with a friendly jab to the shoulder that quite hurt.

Tom carefully removed one grenade from his coat pocket and handed it to McCarthy. The men parted ways with a nod of solidarity. McCarthy headed north towards the first manhole, and Tom turned south.

"Listen for my signal, Joe. I'll be able to take a quick look from back here. Then on my count." he shouted after him, and McCarthy gave him a thumbs up.

When they reached their respective manholes, both men climbed the stairs to the surface and fixed their ears to cutouts, waiting for the vibration of the approaching vehicles. Adrenaline and fear combined with the suffocating stench of the sewer and sweat began to pool on their faces.

CHAPTER 3

The Ambush

"**O**ne final run down the quays, Corporal Jensen, before we head back home to the barracks," grumbled Sergeant Miller, who oversaw the four-army truck patrol.

Their routine objective was to furtively patrol the empty streets at unholy hours in the hopes of spotting the slightest insurrection and then do whatever they deemed necessary to squelch it.

"I've got four bottles stashed under my bunk, Sarge. Four bo'les of liquid magic," hissed the seedy-looking corporal. He nonchalantly gripped the steering wheel with one hand as he maneuvered the second armored vehicle in the line, barely focused on the road ahead. The man was already intoxicated, and despite the sufficient light radiating from the streetlamps and the vehicle's own headlamps, he swerved the chassis of the Seabrook Armored truck rattling the men in the back from side to side as they took the bend.

The first truck interrupted the still of the night as its tires crackled over the rough, cobbled stones, clinking over the other manholes a hundred yards from where Joe stood.

The sergeant smirked. "We'll down some when we get back to the base?"

"My arse has been bloody frozen for the last four hours, Sarge… and still no action. We should 'ave picked up a colleen or two to 'company us back to the barracks, eh Sarge? Jensen continued, slurring his words, "There's no chance of the Major poppin' in tonigh'. We could 'ave 'ad some fun."

Sergeant Miller grinned at the suggestion, lust hazing his eyes. "You're right! There's no chance! Fuckin' bastard thinks we're all bloody vermin anyway. 'we just wants us to play the par' of his li'le soldier boys and dance to 'is tune like 'is mistress. We are only 'ere because we are be'er off serving the king than rottin' in jail like scum." spat Sergeant Miller, his teeth gritted in anger.

"Spo' on Sarge, dead bloody righ'." slurred Corporal Jensen, taking another swig from the bottle.

"So, where we can get ourselves some female comp'ny for tonigh'?" They both snorted as their breath formed little clouds in the eerie chill of the night.

Lost in a daze of whiskey and lust, the corporal blindly trailed the truck in front as he weaved on the road, bleary-eyed from the whisky in his right hand, which he passed every few seconds to the sergeant.

Sergeant Miller groaned as they approached the brewery, "I loathe the sight of Kingsbridge. I hate these flaming carts on the side. Why do they need to put the bloody things here? Corporal, remind me to have a word wif the damn manager of the brewery on Monday. Wait, no! Better yet, we'll knock him up tomorra before he 'eads off to holy mass, shall we?" they both laugh maliciously.

The corporal looked to his sergeant with admiration. These men were rogue, ruthless thugs expunged from British jails solely for these purposes. Some had been convicted of heinous crimes, and they all seemed to share the same roughneck mentality with an inclination to inebriation, philandering, and violence.

As the trucks approached the ambush, Weasel turned to eye the boy, who stood silently next to him.

"How did you manage to shoot the arse of a Tan. That's what I'd like to know. And did the wanker run away like a fretful virgin who'd been caught in the act?" Weasel muttered with a sly smile.

Patrick squinted his eyes in confusion, "What do you mean, sir?"

Weasel laughed at Patrick's innocence, with his hands tucked into the pockets of his trench coat. The more Weasel envisioned the scene, the more he laughed until tears formed in his eyes. Weasel placed both palms flat against Patrick's shoulders and looked him straight in the eyes with a toothy grin. "Patrick, me boy, I won't tell you now. But next Saturday night, how bou' I take you out with me to a little place I know and show you what I mean?"

Patrick looked at Weasel curiously to see if the man was going to elaborate. Weasel only smiled and speculated on such an excursion. How amusing it would be to see the boy go weak in his knees at the sight of the infamous establishment he had in his mind. Despite his age, he knew he could get him in. His charm and sense of humor made people feel comfortable and vulnerable, and it had served him well in his life. Weasel usually got what he wanted.

By the time Patrick had muscled up the courage to ask Weasel for further explanation, he was told to remain quiet. Weasel had spotted the first truck and the first victim of the night as it turned onto Kingsbridge. He signaled with a wave and retreated to the alley, pulling the boy along with him.

On the street, Tom saw the signal, and both men could hear the growling of the approaching lorries and the stench of petrol as it polluted the air around them. McCarthy waited breathlessly in the dark for the signal. Tom, peeking out of his hole, could now see the first vehicle about twenty yards away from McCarthy's manhole. He had to time this perfectly. Tom retreated, pulling the cover back over his manhole, and began counting. He had watched this patrol with Murphy every night for the last two weeks, timing the distance and speed in order to inflict the most damage.

"Thirty, twenty-nine, twenty-eight…ten, nine, eight…three, two, one." As the roar of the lorries passed overhead, Tom banged the cast iron ladder with his pistol and yelled, "Now!"

His partner tightened his grip on the ladder and hoisted himself up until his head touched the cover. Tom replicated the movement under the first truck as it neared his manhole. In the dark, both men simultaneously removed the pins of the Stielhandgranates, which they clasped firmly against their sweaty palms, and pulled down the cutout manholes. In one swift movement, they tossed their grenades under their designated trucks and immediately slid down the stairs like two firemen on a pole and made for their exit tunnel as they had planned. That was where they had stashed their newly acquired Tommy guns.

A deafening explosion, followed by another a couple of seconds later, rattled the ground above them. Tom's Stielhandgranate had exploded under the rear wheels of the first Seabrook Lorry, launching it into the air like a bucking stallion before it landed with an excruciating thud. Pieces of bloody flesh and debris shot through the night sky, bursting into bright streaks of yellow and orange flames, polluting the space in all directions before falling grotesquely limp against the cold, unforgiving cobblestones.

Seconds later, the fourth truck exploded like fireworks against the pitch-black night sky; the vivid yellows illuminated the brewery. For a moment, it almost looked celebratory, save for the gut-wrenching shrieks issuing from the blaze. The third truck stumbled and crashed into the second, which had somehow remained mostly unscathed, probably because the first truck had absorbed almost all the impact of Tom's grenade. The occupants of the second truck had managed to scramble to safety before flames proliferated in every direction. Thick black smoke now congealed in the air, and men staggered from the wreckage, crying in agony as their clothing burned mercilessly.

The perpetrators disappeared like rats into the oblivion of the sewer tunnels, running silently, neither stopping to talk nor even breathe. Even in the tunnel, a decent distance from the ambush, they could sense the heat prickling against their skin and could feel the reverberations of the ground above them. They shivered with uncertainty and excitement.

The Tans had been ensnared. This element of surprise had been their Trojan Horse, and it had served them well once again. In addition to the fatalities, they had successfully destroyed at least three British Army vehicles. Some men lay dead on the road in pools of crimson and shrapnel, while others attempted to drag their limp and wounded bodies from the fire, ignoring the orders that were rolling out from their sergeant.

While the scene of terror unfolded above ground, some distance away, neither Tom nor McCarthy had the luxury of lingering before bullets pierced the vacant sewer, ricocheting off the metal and stone in a constant barrage. Tom and McCarthy returned fire. Each bullet that resulted in a dull thud signified its contact with a softer target. More fatalities. The assailants continued their dash through the tunnel, managing to evade their pursuers until they exited the sewer, armed and breathless, onto what was a bona fide battlefield. Dashing their way into the middle of the conflagration they had created, they stood breathless for a moment, imbibing the scene with awe and without an ounce of remorse. Many of these Tans were recognizable and carried with them a list of atrocities and grievances from people they knew and loved.

They were shocked that they had managed to trigger such a massive demolition. They charged into the middle of the scene, intent on eliminating any remaining targets. Despite an attempted assault from the Tans, who were held up on the other side of the brewery, miraculously, they made it safely to the alley side of the building. The smell of burning flesh and petroleum mingled in the thick, smoky air around them. Three of the trucks were smoldering in angry flames, and the fourth sat vacantly. This marked the destruction of three-quarters of this rogue British patrol.

On the other side of the road, Sergeant Miller hid by the brewery wall. He was left with only twelve soldiers, essentially the survivors of his lorry, the one that didn't explode. He'd seen Sutton and his big man escape to the other side of the building while they were exchanging fire with other assailants across the street by the river. He had no idea how many he was up against. Reluctantly, he'd have to radio for backup.

Three of the men who had survived the third truck had taken off into the sewers, but he had no idea of their whereabouts now. All Miller could do was corral his remaining men against the brewery wall and get them out of the line of fire. From the safety of the other side of the brewery, the one closest to the bridge, Tom and McCarthy scanned the battlefield and easily claimed two more of Miller's men as they attempted to follow their commander and rush towards the brewery for cover.

Tom hadn't expected this many causalities. They had hoped to take down two lorries at best. But the entire street was on fire, and his crew practically decimated the patrol unit. His men were trapped on the other side of this inferno, and retreating to safety now was not an option. He would not abandon or betray his crew. The cold night air bit at his cheeks as the heat from the foul, burning mass of flesh and metal around them rose to meet it.

They withdrew to the alley, where Weasel and Patrick were still tucked away. Weasel had seen Tom and McCarthy scramble to the side of the brewery, and from their hideaway, Weasel had been able to take down two of Miller's men who had tried to sneak around the back of the building and ambush them. Tom was sure the Tans would call for help if they hadn't already, and the Fire Department was bound to be on its way by now. When the British troops arrived, they'd break up and encircle them, and it would be all over. They'd all hang for this. There wasn't much time.

"Weasel! You, Patrick, and McCarthy, get the hell out of here now," said Tom breathlessly as he rounded the alley. "Get out through the alley before they close off all the exits."

"But what about you and Flynn and Shamus?"

"Don't worry about me. I'll find a way to help them. It's an order, lad." Tom said emphatically, but none of them made any move to leave.

"Damn your orders, you eejit. I'm part of an army that never provided me with a uniform. Therefore, I am not obliged to follow any orders. I'm not leaving you or my brother or Flynn here alone."

"Hey, I'm staying too. I didn't sign up for just the easy bits." McCarthy grinned with determination.

They were critically low on time, and Tom knew better than to initiate a futile argument with these two. Weasel suddenly remembered that they had the boy with them, and none of them was willing to jeopardize his life.

"Lad, get out of here as quickly as you can, and don't look back. Go before someone sees you. That's an order!" Weasel looked like a madman, and the boy decided it was best not to argue with him and sped off down the alley faster than a well-bred Irish steeplechaser.

"I'd report the two of you feckers, but to whom? You mad bastards, what in the hell are you thinking," said Tom. But the grins on his friends' faces were unmovable.

"Alright, the Tans are on the other side of the building, as you know. I'm sure they're bloodthirsty as hell by now. We need to get Shamus and Flynn off the bridge before these bastards get to them or the bloody army arrives on the bridge. Weasel, you're the fastest. McCarthy and I will create a diversion, and you run. Stick close to the fire for cover. Get everyone into the river if you must, but head that way, away from the bridge. We will stay here and hold them off as long as we can. Just get yourselves to Maggie's. We'll meet up there. Weasel, go, go now!"

Weasel took off like a shot. Seconds later, Tom squinted, and through the smoke, he could make out the faint outline of British uniforms. They were already on the bridge. But Weasel had already gone, and it would be too dangerous to call him back now with two Tans already in pursuit. Tom and McCarthy entered the battlefield and began firing wildly at anything that moved, trying to give Weasel as much cover as possible. Weasel sprinted like lightning across the street, sticking close to the fire for cover as Tom had suggested.

When they could no longer see him, they retreated to the building.

"If they don't get out of there now, the army will pick them off from the bridge," Tom whispered nervously. "Come on, Weasel."

"Can't those two eejits see them coming?" said McCarthy with frustration.

"Wait, hold, I see them!" Said Tom, leaning out from the wall. "Jaysus! They're shooting up the other side of the Brewery wall."

Shamus and Flynn had climbed the ladders near the bridge and had been exchanging fire with the Tans, who was hiding on the other side of the brewery wall. It was likely their cover and not sheer luck that had made it possible for Tom and McCarthy to get to safety in the first place. As Weasel reached the other side of the street, they also took out both the Tans that had followed him, and Weasel scrambled over the wall. He had made it.

Gunshots were fired from the other side of the bridge. The British had spotted them, and Shamus and Flynn suddenly realized they were trapped. If they stayed where they were, they were dead men. Tom couldn't see that another troop of soldiers had amassed further down the river, sealing their only exit. They could try swimming, but they were essentially surrounded. Shamus began to panic and yelled out to Tom, hoping his voice would be heard across the battlefield. "Tom, we need help. We are trapped."

Tom called back in Gaelic. They couldn't risk telegraphing any plan of escape, no matter how reckless or stupid.

"Joe and I will try to get their truck and back it up in your direction. When it's in position, climb over the wall. Joe and I will cover you."

"Got it," came the response in Gaelic from the river.

The British troops were closing in and began to exchange fire. A few negligible shots were fired back and forth until one pierced Flynn's neck. Blood instantly gushed through his shirt collar and scarf, and he fell backwards into the slimy river mud. "No, please, God no!" screamed Shamus, reaching for the man.

Flynn was dead instantly. Weasel had to pull his brother forcibly away from the body and push him along the wall until they could press themselves into a little niche. From the niche, they could still see blood pour from Flynn's neck as it mingled with river mud. His eyes stared lifelessly at the night sky.

Tom had almost made it to the truck when McCarthy was hit in the back, falling forward almost at his feet. Tom quickly aimed and shot his pursuer. He heaved the large man into the truck as Joe groaned in pain. British soldiers had now entered through the alley, and the Tans had relinquished their position at the brewery wall and disappeared. He had no more time.

Men shouted, guns fired, and small explosions pierced the night air. Roaring towards them came the British truck, "Get in!" yelled

Tom. Several soldiers were now in pursuit. Shamus took one final look at Flynn's body; his blood had escaped into little channels in the muddy riverbank and mingled with the mud. Flynn had always loved the river; now, this would forever be his grave. It was almost poetic. Shamus thought that this man would die right here on the banks of this river, on the land he had loved so well.

As Weasel and Shamus crawled into the truck, McCarthy moaned loudly. It was then that Tom noticed that not one, but three bullet holes had pierced his coat. The smoke mixed with the smell of blood, and Tom was suddenly in shock.

"Drive for God's sake, Tom…drive!" screamed Weasel, punching him in the arm. Tom snapped into motion, and the truck jerked forward. Weasel took the window, and Shamus took the back, shooting anyone who dared pursue them. Tom maneuvered the truck up an alleyway heading for Dame Street. McCarthy groaned with each bump in the road, and soon, his breathing became labored. Weasel and Tom tried to comfort him in those final minutes, but Joe McCarthy passed silently into the night somewhere along that road.

When the stolen vehicle approached the corner of the alley, they instantly recognized the black berets of five Black & Tans surrounding a corpse. Two stood off to the side laughing while the others stabbed the body with their rifle bayonets. Young Patrick's curly strawberry-blond hair was unmistakable, even at a distance.

The Tans thought nothing of the approaching truck deeming it was one of theirs, and continued to laugh and dance about like beasts at a séance. Weasel cried out at the sight of Patrick. Tom said nothing but pressed his foot on the accelerator and tightened his grip on the steering wheel. His eyes narrowed on his targets, and Shamus took his cue and laid flat in the back of the truck. This was retribution. After the truck had rolled them over, Shamus emptied the contents of his weapon on what remained of the three men. The other two managed to escape into the crack between two buildings.

"He was just a young lad," Weasel muttered and swiftly wiped away a tear that spilt down his cheek. As they continued down Dame Street, the two escapees pursued them on foot. The fire was exchanged, and Tom saw Tans fall into the road. As soon as they were in the clear, Tom stopped the vehicle about fifty yards from Trinity College.

"We get out here," he said to Weasel. "It's too conspicuous. Take Shamus and meet me at Maggie's later. I must get a message to Murphy first. But before we leave, we torch the truck." he choked as he spoke. "This way, they won't get a hold of McCarthy's body." And we can give him a proper hero's death, like men of old."

"Yes," said Weasel solemnly. "Let's do that."

Weasel jumped out and called to his brother, but when no reply came, both Tom and Weasel rounded the vehicle. Blood oozed from a small hole over Shamus' left eye. Like Flynn, his eyes stared vacantly at the night sky, but a peaceful expression remained on his face. It was almost a smile. He must have left this earth feeling vindicated, or at least that's what Tom would say later about Shamus.

Weasel climbed into the back of the truck, took his brother into his arms, and shook him vigorously.

"No, God, no! Shamus, get up. Don't do this to me. Please…wake up!" screamed Weasel frantically as tears spilt from his eyes.

When Shamus remained motionless, Weasel took his brother's blood-covered face and held him in his lap. His hands trembling in shock, and his cries pierced the silence. He was nearing hysteria.

Tom climbed onto the truck, grabbed Weasel by his collar, and slapped him hard. He did not mean to be cruel, but they were being pursued, and if they stayed here any longer, they would suffer the same fate as their friends and brother.

Weasel's lips quivered, and he sobbed. "My brother Tom…he's gone… now there's only two of us left …you and me."

Tom snapped at Weasel, "Well, I'm not ready to die yet, and I sure as hell aren't going to let you die either. Shamus would want you to live, Weasel. We've got to get out of here."

"But I can't leave Shamus here by himself, Tom!" Weasel exclaimed.

"You have to, Weasel," Tom said emphatically. Weasel had become numb and bereft of words. He allowed Tom to physically pull him off the truck without any resistance. Tom ripped off a piece of his shirt, opened his lighter, doused the fabric with lighter fluid, and lit it. He lifted the truck's hood and dropped the burning wad onto the already overheated engine. As he dragged Weasel away from the vehicle, he mumbled a few short words of prayer.

Weasel's tears never ran dry, and he kept looking back at his brother lying in the back of the truck until they neared Aston Quay. Then they picked up speed, and Weasel ran dutifully alongside Tom. He did not know what else to do but followed Tom's orders. As they crossed the Halfpenny Bridge towards Capel Street, they heard the explosion and silently slipped into the safety of Maggie's Place.

CHAPTER 4

Dublin Castle

Despite the early morning hour, a light had been turned on in Major Warren T. Siddley's office at Dublin Castle. The sun was just rising, and dew clung to the windowpane. News of the vicious blow had spread like wildfire, and all personnel had been alerted. Sutton's stunt last night was sure to drive a new wave of hostility and resentment towards the British military. Tom Sutton was to be arrested on sight, and the Major was under scrutiny for the actions of some of the men in his charge.

British army personnel officer Sergeant Armstrong, a middle-aged Scotsman with broad shoulders and a do-good attitude sat behind a desk tucked away in the farthest corner of the room, away from the drafty windows and opposite the Major. His brass standard-issue military desk clock sat prominently to the left of his desk while a large black British army radio dominated the remainder of the space. He had been sitting here like this for the last four hours listening, headphones on, fingers glued to the dials in front of him.

On the opposite side of the room, Major Siddley's shadow on the wall behind him rendered a brooding silhouette as he stroked his moustache thoughtfully. Six men under his command now stood before him solemnly, with their heads hung low, their berets in hand.

This was not the kind of commission Major Siddley had ever wanted. In fact, he preferred that peace be reinstated so he could return to England. He was a gentleman officer of some repute. He had no desire to referee a civil war; at forty-two, he was still too young to retire. The events of last night had left him conflicted. Sutton and his gang had killed more than twenty men and had destroyed four of their armored trucks. But the Tans had been ruthless, as they always were, and were no doubt still bloodthirsty for revenge. Capturing Sutton as soon as possible was the best and only solution to restore any order and prevent further violence.

This had to be done systematically and cautiously. Tom was a hero to the Irish resistance. One wrong move, even a slight one, could lead to unfathomable consequences and more lives lost. He perused the men before him. Some sported grazes and bloodied noses; others bore blotches of ashes and singed hair from the recent catastrophe. These were the escapees of the fray. The Major was angry, and not one of the six men dared utter a word as the tension in the air plugged up their throats.

Major Siddley had already fought in two wars. He was a decorated soldier, having earned himself a Military Cross for bravery in the Battle of the Frontiers, where he had also taken a bullet to the hip at the Battle of Amiens that had brought him home early. He had only accepted this commission because he had no choice in the matter, but he quietly disapproved of the unconventional "warfare" perpetrated by the Black and Tans. He had earned the respect of colleagues and fellow British soldiers for his moral convictions, but the Black and Tans held it against him shamelessly. Operating under these circumstances had made him irritable, demanding, and often very stern.

Siddley's simmering agitation finally boiled over, and he propelled his chair against the wall with a loud thud, reaffirming what these men already knew of their superior. He did not care for them or their tactics. Armstrong jolted in his seat across the room and removed his headphones to watch the drama unfold.

The Major approached a seedy little man with scruffy hair and dirty fingernails. He had an arrogant look about him that Siddley didn't tolerate in his soldiers. Despite being genteel and well-educated, Siddley was tall with an athletic build. He could appear quite threatening when he had a mind to be. He stopped in front of the man and bellowed in his face.

"Can someone please tell me how three men got run over by their own damn truck?"

"I dunno," the man said dismissively as he looked down at the floor and shuffled his feet nervously.

"And how on earth did that happen? Did the lorry fall from the sky? How do three of you idiots get run down by one of our own lorries?"

"Coz we thought they wuz our mates, sir. We never dreamt...."

Siddley interrupted angrily, "Dreamt? You do realize that this is warfare, corporal. If I had had the slightest bit of a clue as to your ineptitude or general lack of any moral code, I would have never deployed you to patrol the city in the first place."

"But sir, we were going about just fine...."

"Don't you dare try and defend yourself, corporal! And where in tarnation was your sergeant during all this?"

"Wif me and boys 'ere and then la'er 'e was shot by one of them when we were chasing the truck, sir. He almost got me too, 'it me right 'ere in the shoulde' but I killed 'im wif a bullet right to 'is 'ead." he said flatly.

"And where is this notorious sergeant now...Miller, isn't it?" " 'es dead." piped another man.

Siddley said nothing but continued to pace in front of them. None dared move or even breathe. The room remained thick and unyielding despite the cheerful morning sun that now broke through the windows.

Muttering under his breath yet audible enough for the Tans to hear, Siddley mused, "I can only blame myself for this mistake. What was I thinking when I made that fool a sergeant? ...nothing but uncivilized criminals."

Reclaiming his abused chair from the corner of the room, the Major slumped into it, and he ran both of his hands through his light brown hair, which had greyed slightly at the temples. For the first time in his career, he wished he was somewhere else as visions of the ambush invaded his mind. Without the Major's gaze fixed upon them, the men began to look nervously at one other.

This was just the trigger that could spark a wave of insurrection. A spark big enough perhaps to ignite a blood lust for retribution among the populace. When news got out about the brutal killings perpetrated on their side, there was sure to be another rebellion, and it had all been on his watch.

He had to be careful and calculated in his response, and time was not on their side. He pushed back a few loose strands of hair that hung over his eye and straightened his lapel. Slowly and methodically, he took in the men standing before him, allowing his gaze to scrutinize each one of them.

"I gather while you and your sergeant were preoccupied with escaping our runaway Vehicle, you wouldn't have perchance recognized any of these reactionaries.

"Yes sir," the corporal replied with confidence, straightening up as he spoke.

"Who were they, corporal?"

"Sutton, a big man named McCarthy and a scrawny looking chap who goes by the name of Weasel and 'is bruva…he's the one I shot in the 'ead." the corporal declared proudly.

Siddley ignored the last statement. This was all the confirmation he needed. "You're absolutely sure?" asked Siddley, rounding on the man.

But before the corporal could respond, a smarmy private named Smith stepped forward with his arms folded at his back and answered, "Yes sir, I can affirm that the corporal is right. I saw them plain as day, and it was them alright - Sutton, McCarthy, and Weasel. And I fink we got the big one, though…McCarthy… back by Kingsbridge."

Sutton had been on a short list of wanted men for at least a year now. And the Major was acutely aware of how many times the man had escaped arrest and even death. His evasiveness had tarnished the Major's reputation.

"Armstrong."

"Yes sir." said the Scotsman, standing to attention.

"Thomas Edward Sutton? … has any of our information given us any clues as to his whereabouts in the past? He has to reside somewhere."

"No sir," squeaked Sergeant Armstrong, who had remained dutifully silent during this interrogation, from his desk in the corner. "We did track down a piece of property near Enniskerry a few months ago that's in his wife's name, but they have not been seen there for ages…not even the wife or son. He has been spotted in Dublin on occasion. But he holds no property, rent or otherwise, and he moves about frequently."

"Well, Sergeant, you have exactly six hours to bring me Sutton's location. Understood? And I suggest you question this lot before they depart. Get a description of all of them. I want positive results, and I want them today."

"Yes sir," Sergeant Armstrong said solemnly, giving the Major a classic salute and returning furiously to the piles of paper on his desk. Only the rhythmic creaks of the ceiling fan above and the click of the Major's boots on the wood floor permeated the silence as the men awaited their orders.

"Let's assume that we can muster up the competence to locate this one elusive man and actually arrest him. Am I right to assume that you'd all want to partake in his torment as retribution for the demise of your comrades?" The men before him looked hungrily at each other and nodded in agreement, imagining the injuries they could inflict on Tom Sutton.

Bellowing, the Major shot a warning across their bows. "Know this! Your craven display last night disgusts me. Not only did you suffer massive casualties because of your drunkenness and incompetence. But one assailant was shot six times in the chest after he was already dead in a riverbed, and another, a mere boy who didn't appear to even be a part of the attack, was bayoneted to death for sport. That's not how we operate in the King's Army." Siddley squinted his eyes at each of the men.

"Now get out of my sight before I do something I regret. See Sergeant Armstrong before you leave, and then confine yourselves to your barracks until further notice. That's a direct order."

After each man had given his testimony to Armstrong under Major Siddley's scrutinizing gaze, they escaped out his office door one by one. The Major sat back in his chair and rubbed his aching hip. He sometimes swore that when his temper flared, he aggravated his old injury. As much as he wanted Sutton apprehended, he worried about the terrorist-like tactics the Tans had begun to employ across the country with more frequency in the name of the crown. Sutton was their natural enemy, of course, but the war had rules of conduct, and they seemed to be losing control of it to these hired hands. Sadly, even soldiers in his own army had chosen to turn a blind eye to their violence to ensure victory at all costs.

The Tans' collective rage exploded upon their return to their barracks. Here in their own digs, they huddled between a set of bunks and swore an oath of loyalty.

"To hell with the Major and the la di fucking dah English Army... we will deal with that bastard Sutton on our terms," the corporal spat.

Now that the corporal was their sole superior after the rebel attack, Private Smith could not refrain from stepping up to fuel the burning anger among them.

"I swear my fingers are itching to strangle that Sutton as soon as I see him... I'll make him pay."

The corporal's face, ruddy with rage, reaffirmed. "We will make him pay, Smith. Don't worry about that. When it's time, we will barge in through 'is door, as instructed by the good Major. But there will be no arrest, and there will be no handcuffs. Instead, we will execute our plan. We will deliver that bastard's limp body slashed and bleeding right to the Major's feet, and then we will hear what 'e has to say about our soldiering, won't we?"

After a moment of silence, the corporal disappeared under his bunk bed and pulled out a dirty box. Dusting it off, he opened the lid and pulled out four bottles of whiskey. At the sight of this liquid gold, all the men sat in a circle and admired him as if he was a magician who had just pulled a live rabbit out of his hat.

The bottles were passed around, and as they clinked, the men chanted in solidarity, "To Sarge Miller and our mates. We will make sure to make Sutton and Weasel pay for each drop of your blood."

The bottles circulated as the cheap liquor was devoured in big gulps. The more they drank and the more tired they got, the more resolute they became, and the desire for revenge surged within them. After collapsing in their allocated bunks in a near-drunken stupor, each man replayed the chaos of the last several hours in their mind as visions of the flaming blaze and screams of departed souls tormented their sleep.

* * * *

Armstrong had spent all morning sifting through street maps and communicating with army field agents by radio, trying to gather Sutton's whereabouts. But despite his relentless efforts, he had failed. As promised, when the clock's arms pointed at the twelve, Major Siddley materialized in the doorway, demanding Sutton's location.

When Armstrong couldn't deliver, The Major ordered him off the radio and out into the streets of Dublin to gather informants. Someone had to have seen Sutton. The large man took his orders graciously, glad to depart the stifling office and the Major's foreboding presence. He feared that he would face disciplinary action if he came up short-handed, but he couldn't deny that he was glad to be free of the Major and the castle for at least the next hour or two.

By late afternoon, Armstrong returned with flushed cheeks and tentative optimism. He nodded with a minute amount of self-respect as he ushered in the informants and lined them up where the Tans had stood disgraced only twelve hours before.

It was a motley crew, to be sure. Of the five, only one seemed remotely put together. Their clothes and faces were worn and battered from a hard life on the city streets. These were opportunists, deal makers, and snitches, not people who anyone might call upstanding. They had no allegiance to either side, and that was clear as they stood haphazardly before Siddley, switching from one foot to the other and smiling amongst themselves, unafraid of his presence. Siddley's dour demeanor emanating from the corner desk had failed to have any threatening effect upon them at all. He tried another tact. Siddley calmly rose and paced methodically back and forth in front of them for a few minutes before speaking. They only watched him and smiled awkwardly at each other.

"Now, we might be paying the King's good money in exchange for any information that may be beneficial. But in the past, some of you good gentlemen have furnished us with some worthless rubbish. So, if you aren't here to provide me with the answers I want, get out now!"

Siddley, for all his measured rhetoric, knew that these men might be his only chance to stop this game of hide-and-seek with Sutton and quash this uprising once and for all. Seeing the smiles on the men's idle faces infuriated him. Did they think this was a game? With purpose and authority, Siddley held all their attention and, in a half whisper, commanded. "I will also add - anyone who withholds information shall be held liable. Which, gentlemen, means treason. We all know what that means."

The men now straightened up, and any levity amongst them escaped like an embarrassed child through the crack in the door. They shuffled in discomfort, looking at their feet, hands, or anywhere that wasn't Siddley's piercing blue eyes as he glowered over them. These informants knew that they had what he wanted, but they also knew that being a snitch was an irrevocable decision. The Major had no clue of what the I.R.A. was capable of. If their traitorous behavior was discovered, they would be tracked down and executed by Sinn Féin before any British judge could charge them with "treason". These men were at the edge of a precipice Siddley couldn't understand.

Siddley waited patiently until one of the men, named Moore, the most put together of these bottom feeders, decided to act as representative and verbalized their collective fears. "Your honor, Sir, are you aware that the I.R.A. previously shot a man dead on the steps of

Saint Patrick's Cathedral in the grandeur of New York City for being a traitor? Just because he had given up the whereabouts of one of their members?"

Another chimed in. "I heard about that, too. He was promised a safe passage, but it turned out to be a trap."

As a series of murmurs issued from the group, the Major stopped them. He pulled out his revolver and placed it ceremoniously on his desk.

"You see that gun, gentleman? I assure you that our conversation stays here. And anyone who even tries to come after you will have to deal with me personally. I also promise you that you'll have the full protection of the British Army."

After his speech, he ordered Armstrong to keep the men out in the hallway and allow one in at a time for a personal interview with him. The interrogations went on for hours until the castle lay still and mostly dark, save for the singular lamp light emanating from Siddley's office. Armstrong's desk clock clicked 21:30. It had taken them a full twenty-four hours since the ambush to track down Sutton, but they had succeeded. They had a verifiable address, Sutton's residence, a little house in Palmerstown.

The Major pulled a cigarette from his case and lit it. The smoke climbed wistfully through the chilly air, and he relaxed in his chair, exhaling a ring of smoke. He had earned this, but now he had to be systematic about the arrest. Armstrong waited expectantly at the doorway for further instructions.

Siddley took another pull and then addressed him. "Give them something to eat, and then let them all go. But make sure they're taken out in separate trucks and deposited somewhere discreetly in the city for their own protection, as for that fellow Moore. Lock him up for a couple of days. Tell them it's for drunk and disorderly conduct. That stoolie gave up Sutton's entire existence for twenty-five pounds. I shouldn't have wasted my time talking to the rest of them. But I don't trust the man; he could just as easily be playing us, and I wouldn't put it past him to turn tail and go right to the IRA for a sum. We need to reach Sutton before anyone else does. Once we have him in our remand, you can let Moore go."

"Very well, sir," said Armstrong. "Will there be anything else, sir?"

"I want you to handle his arrest, Armstrong, but wait until the morning. I don't want Sutton harmed. And if you must take along those ruffians from last night for backup, they are not to lay a hand on the man. I want him presented to me in full mind and body. Understood?"

"Why do you care, sir… if you don't mind me asking?" said Armstrong, speaking a little out of character.

"Well, I'm sure, as a Scotsman, you can relate to Sutton's cause, Sergeant, can't you? How many times has Scotland been invaded over the centuries? You gain a certain perspective when you've fought in wars. Armstrong, you remember the Battle of the Frontiers. Sutton believes we have invaded his country and that we are seeking to impose our ideologies on his countrymen. And there is no denying that the Black and Tans have committed atrocities in the name of the crown that any man would find hard to forgive."

"Sir, as a Scotsman, I think I understand exactly what you mean." replied the sergeant sympathetically in his thick Glasgow accent.

"Very well then. You are uniquely equipped to handle this delicate situation, then Armstrong. Arrest Sutton and imprison him. Unfortunately for him, he will have to wait and see if Ireland ever gets liberated from behind the bars of Kilmainham Jail. But Armstrong, if he resists arrest or presents any real threat to my men, you have my permission to shoot him."

"Yes, sir," Armstrong saluted and left the room. In the hallway, Siddley could hear him rounding up the informants as he had ordered. He smiled and finished the last pull of the cigarette. He liked Armstrong. He reminded him of his Scottish grandfather. He trusted that Armstrong would soon have Sutton in custody, and he would finally get to meet the man face to face.

CHAPTER 5

Maggie's Place

Diffused morning light penetrated through the fabric of the thick ruby muslin adhered to the makeshift attic windows of Maggie's place. Umber tentacles streaked the darkness, evincing a color reminiscent of the bloodshed from the battle two nights before. This new anticipated dawn had failed these freedom fighters. The aspiring, burning desire for progress, for a free Ireland, had come as anticipated, but it felt like a pyrrhic victory, hollow and lusterless. Thomas Edward Sutton and his remaining compatriots knew that their holocaust they had inflicted serious damage on the Black and Tans two nights before. It had been splattered on every newspaper, and people still murmured in hush whispers in the street. And while they could embrace the victory, the personal loss seemed far more devastating in the light of day.

Tom thought about what dramatic change the passage of time can wield in a solitary day. They had last gathered here together the morning of the attack forty-eight hours ago. Joe, Patrick, Weasel, Flynn, Shamus, and Tom, unable to contain their eagerness, had devoured a full Irish breakfast of eggs, beans, bacon, and sausage, complete with fresh soda bread and marmalade. Maggie, a stalwart ally, had been happy to oblige, and the money always helped.

All the men had slurped tea and eaten heartily in the comfort and warmth of their discreet accommodations, nary a thought of night's events ahead of them. They laughed and shared a brother-hood that made them more than posse. They were friends.

Now, from his vantage point on the makeshift bed in the attic hideaway, Tom couldn't divert his eyes from the blood-red muslin that now taunted him. He searched his mind for the plans that Murphy had proposed two nights before, looking for the flaw. He exhaled deeply. They had executed their plans alright, he thought. Their ambush had successfully crippled half of the British platoon, most of whom were Black & Tans. But that meant nothing against the human loss, their human loss.

Weasel lay next to him, like an old dog bereaved and defeated. Gone was his wry smile and quick wit. Time was a cruel assailant. Only two mornings before, they were here, breathing, laughing… living. Now, only Tom and Weasel had escaped the scene of ruin. It seemed surreal and vacuous. Tom rose slowly and approached the window cautiously. In an attempt to survey the streets below, he bent low to peek through a slit in the window.

Tom was glad that Maggie had a window in the attic hideaway, even if it had wooden planks nailed across it. But he loathed the red cloth that stretched over the gaps. Squinting through between the planks, Tom judged the time to be around 8:00 A.M. on Monday morning. His watch had been destroyed in the fight last night, so he had to rely on instinct.

He and Weasel had been holed up here for over twenty-four hours now after slipping in the back door around three am on Sunday morning, covered in ash and blood. Murphy had sent word to them to stay put until the search for them had subsided a little, and then he'd figure out how to get them out of the city. But Tom worried about his tickets for the ship. The voyage left this afternoon, and he had to get home.

Sunrays crashed against the building like a beacon, telegraphing their hideaway to the passersby below. He tiptoed his way back across the room and slouched back down beside Weasel on the horsehair mattress. There was no lamp, no light, or even a candle to brighten the attic. The only sources of light were the sun rays that penetrated the red material and managed to escape around the wood planks that barred the window.

In this dim light, Tom could barely make out the stains of blood on his skin anymore. While they had both slept most of Sunday away out of sheer exhaustion. Tom had awoken this morning, fully alert and agitated. He had been pacing the attic since dawn like a caged animal while Weasel continued to sleep fitfully on the bed. Maggie had brought him up a basin and some soap to wash with, as well as some food and water for the fugitives.

For the first time in his life, Tom felt horribly alone. Bereft and alone, without even their shadows to comfort them in this solitude. Weasel awoke with a groan. His already unruly hair was matted to his face with tears and blood, and his deep blue eyes were red and swollen. He turned his ruddy face towards Tom. Tom sat on the edge of the bed and patted his shoulder in earnest. He hung his head in his hands, low between his knees, as if in prayer or maybe exasperation. Weasel joined him, and the two men sat in silence like that for some time.

Opposite them, two dusty wooden chairs faced them, looking forlorn and busted as if mimicking their predicament. "The irony of our inner state," Tom mused to himself. He recognized that Weasel had suffered the greater loss – his only brother, Shamus. And maybe it was for that reason that Tom had tried to stay close to Weasel on this pungent mattress for two nights now. It was a show of solidarity for a man he had loved too, and Weasel appreciated the gesture.

Weasel and Shamus had been inseparable for as long as Tom could remember. Even though Weasel had always been known as the jokester, his older brother Shamus could make them all belly laugh like no other. Being four years younger, Weasel remembered how he had followed his older brother around as a child like an annoying fly, often earning a smack across the ears for his constant pestering. But it was Mick O'Donnell's bloody lip that won Shamus over in the end. Weasel was the village hothead, and at the ripe old age of eight, he had given Mick a bloody lip after hearing him mock Shamus to some older boys. A deep respect and solidarity were earned that day, and from then on, they have been inseparable. Seamus had been Weasel's protector (when it suited him) and his partner in crime. He had always been more calculated and measured. He had always been the one with the plan, with the forethought.

Weasel couldn't stop his mind from reliving the bayonet stabbing of the young lad and Seamus' knee-jerk reaction to avenge the child. And now his better half was gone in an instant just like that. It was unfathomable.

But in his own loss, Weasel was reminded that Tom still had a wife and son. That was surely enough motivation for Tom to go on with his life despite their losses. But he had nothing. How was he to go on living his life when the strongest memory he could conjure was the last smile on his brother's corpse?

This was the fate they had all signed up for. But when salvation could only be attained by departing this world, the bereaved were left to pick up the pieces. Shamus, he supposed, was in some ethereal place, but Weasel swore that if he intended him to go on living, he would never allow his death to be in vain. The tear drought expunged one single drop as it slowly spilt from Weasel's eye and slid down his cheek. And then, one after another, the floodgates reopened. As he tried to wipe them away furiously with the back of his hand, he noticed, for the first time, his brother's dried blood on his fingers and knuckles.

Like a madman, Weasel examined his hands, sleeves, and trousers. The red splotches were all over him. All grizzly reminders of a brother that was no more. His lips trembled at the sight, and his chest heaved deeply in inconsolable sobs. He turned frantically and started smashing his hands furiously into the mattress in exasperation as he cried Shamus' name into the eerie silence. Tom watched helplessly as Weasel's body shivered, and heaving sobs escaped his body into the forgiving mattress.

He thought he had to stop this noise, or they would be found out. Grabbing him forcefully by the shoulders and gritting his teeth, Tom stared into his watery eyes. "Keep it down, man. We can't give away our hideaway...think about Shamus... you owe him that, at least." Weasel saw the reality of their predicament in Tom's panicked stare and sucked in a sob.

Patting him on the shoulder, Tom rose and made his way back to the window, hoping to catch a glimpse of someone familiar. Maybe Murphy was keeping an eye out and sending help? Anything to take them from this purgatory. But he saw nothing. Looking back at Weasel, now lying face down on the bed, Tom watched as the clenched muscles in his back rose and fell in quietly resigned sobs. He became acutely aware of the growing lump in his own throat.

Tom was a vigilant man and knew one moment of carelessness now could cost them. He knew that he had to somehow motivate Weasel out of this despondence without being callous. He patted his foot against the floor anxiously and bit the corner of his lip. He ripped a piece of the red muslin from the window planks to get a better view of the street.

Focus on something else, Tom, before you end up next to Weasel on the bed crying too. Focus dammit! He told himself.

He juggled his position by the window so he could see down Capel Street. The morning bustle was in full effect. The lampposts were no longer illuminated. Gleeful and glum children made their way to school, satchels in hand, while women flitted to and from the market carrying baskets of produce or pushing babies in carriages. Horse carts passed by carrying supplies, and shopkeepers swept the pavements outside their storefronts. Tough men rolled barrels into the pub as smirking adolescents smoked on the street corner. Businessmen waited patiently for the tram at the end of the street while reading the front page of the morning paper, which could only be about them. Did they think he was a hero or a terrorist, he wondered? But all Tom wanted to be right now anonymous, like those people on the street below, so he could get home to Grace and Sean undetected.

His confidence had begun to wane. They hadn't received word from Murphy since they had arrived, and he was beginning to lose hope that Murphy could even get them out. Maybe Murphy had been arrested?

Grace is my compass, and Sean is my anchor, he kept repeating to himself. *Grace is my compass, and Sean is my anchor.* He sucked back any tears that had dared to escape and refastened the cloth back over the crack, and turned to face Weasel.

Weasel had stopped crying and was staring blankly at the edge of the bed. Tom wanted to comfort him, but he gawked awkwardly at his boots covered in char and blood, another memento of the battle. All he could hear now was the noise from the street below as vehicles sputtered, horses clopped, and people chattered.

The hollow within them filled the space, engulfing them. Tom wasn't sure he would have been able to leave behind his beloved. If it had been Grace or Sean, he could have walked away and saved himself. The act of self-preservation could seem so selfish. He pushed the image from his mind but recognized that Weasel must be battling an overwhelming sense of guilt for leaving his brother.

Clanging and loud voices under the floorboards forced Tom to his feet. It was only the patrons of the establishment banging about. Breakfast was being served. His stomach grumbled as the aroma of eggs and bacon wafted up through the floorboards. He shuffled back to the bed and sat beside Weasel.

"Weasel, there's nothing I can say that will bring them back. But they were warriors Weasel. They knew the risks."

"You just don't understand the loss, Sutton. He was my brother...my only kin."

"I know, but we all volunteered for this. It could have been any of us. And yes, Shamus wasn't my brother, but they were my friends, and they were like brothers to me. I may never know the depth of your pain, but God Damnit Weasel. I wasn't going to just leave you there to die, too.

"Well, you should have."

"None of them would have forgiven me for that, and you know it...especially Shamus."

Weasel turned away and began to sob again.

Tom rose and walked over to the broken chair and kicked it. "Weasel, you have to snap out of this. I have lost men before, good men...it's fuckin' shit, alright. But life will not stop to grant us more time. You and I are alive right now, and we must go on. I need you, alright."

There was silence as Weasel bowed his head shamefully Tom changed the subject. "I'm figuring it's about nine o'clock.

What do you think?" Weasel shrugged his shoulders

"Given the rumpus Maggie's wreaking downstairs, I'd say that all of Dublin knows by now.

"…so, Maggie will want us out, I gather."

"To hell with her," Tom said flippantly. "Murphy has paid her more than she makes in a month. And let's face it, if it weren't for us, this rat-infested place would scare away the customers." Weasel had to smirk because it was inherently true.

"Weasel, I really am so sorry about Shamus. But he gave up his life to save us. That's the ultimate sacrifice. He was a good man…you should be very proud."

"You know Tom, Shamus fancied a lady down the street from ours."

"That scoundrel. He never said anything about it." Tom smiled wryly.

"I caught him off-guard one day when the eejit was grinning like a looney. His head was bowed down, so I thought he was blathered. But then I looked out the window and saw a petite colleen waving at him. Can you believe it? He was blushing like a schoolboy."

"I can't believe it." chuckled Tom, glad to see that Weasel had found a good memory to cling to.

"Oh no… he really fancied that girl. Went out to meet her like a young Romeo in the night. See, her father was strict and against the courtship. And you know, even though Shamus was known for his temper, that lass had him wrapped around her finger. After breakfast on the morning of the skirmish, when we were leaving, he told me he was going to ask her father for her hand. He said she would be the only woman to mother his children and all."

Weasel laughed and then paused solemnly. "How… how will I face the girl, Tom?"

Both men looked at each other. So much regret, wasted life, and wasted love. Each rubbed away tears. Weasel cleared his throat and sucked in deeply.

"Ah shite …bullocks, I should be cherishing how big the bastard turned out to be. He's gonna be a right legend, my dear friend" And just like that, Weasel switched gears, like he had purged all the grief from his body. "So, we cannot sit here anymore, especially if Shamus wanted me to live."

Tom welcomed his friend's exigency and nodded. He pulled out his last two cigarettes from his pocket and offered Weasel one. As he flicked his lighter, he was instantly taken back to the truck and the funeral pyre they had left in their wake. At least they had given them a heroes' burial.

The two men puffed their smokes in silence, exhaling deliberately. Tom closed his eyes and let the nicotine calm his nerves, and this time, when the ghostly visions of his partners invaded his mind, they were standing outside the brewery, smiling.

"Alright, Weasel. I'm sure after last night's success, the whole British army is after us. We haven't had a word for Murphy or anyone else, and I've been scanning the streets below for three hours, waiting for a sign. He is either arrested, dead, or he's expecting us to assume the backup plan."

Which is?

Get to Broadstone. He said he'd have a car waiting there for us if all else failed. It's our only option. Better than sitting here rotting away."

"But won't they be on to us by now?"

"If they knew we were here, they would have come here already. Maggie hasn't heard a word. So, I suppose they had to do some debriefing yesterday, and they'll be on the hunt today. The sooner we get out of Dublin, the better."

"I agree. Easy!"

"I'm not just here for the easy bits." McCarthy had said.

Tom closed his eyes and took a long breath in before whispering to himself, "Thank you for saving my life, Joe. I'll never forget it."

* * * *

Back at headquarters, Armstrong was rolling out orders to his platoon, showing them an authoritative arrest warrant for Thomas Edward Sutton. The Corporal and ten of his men, including his newest fan, Private Smith had been commanded to surround Sutton's residence. They didn't express any outward excitement, but their inner thirst for revenge pulsed through them. They were set to leave in an hour's time for Palmerstown.

CHAPTER 6

Part 1: Coming Home

She stared at the new morning sky and then lovingly at the little boy walking by her side, his thick black hair whipping in the breeze. This was the day that Grace had longed for; she could almost taste it…the end of this chapter of their lives. News of last night's conflict had already travelled from Dublin. She had gathered more pieces of information through the down-face murmurs of neighbors on her way to early mass that morning. She was comforted to hear affirmation amidst the whispers that Tom and Weasel had indeed escaped alive. She listened hard for news of the others but couldn't make out any details. She was happy to be back in Lough Tay, where Tom would rejoin her. She felt safer here.

After church, the parishioners openly decried the violence in and around the church itself. But upon leaving, she couldn't help hearing the whispers of excitement as some debated if this was a turn of the tide for Ireland. She felt liberated. Even though she still received some stares and scowls from the majority of the villagers, who knew who she was, they would never give up one of their own, despite their disapproval. As they veered past the pub on their return home, she had to crack a wry smile as she heard a crowd of men cheering for the cause. She swore she saw someone tip a hat to Thomas Sutton. Her Thomas Sutton. She gripped Sean's hand tightly and allowed herself to breathe in the glorious anticipation.

He would be home soon, and they would pack up the car, shut the cottage door once and for all and set off for their new life in America. And not a moment too soon, she thought, for she feared for Tom's safety in the wake of last night's events. His name was becoming infamous. For a second, she thought of her parents. Would they want to see her again, especially now that Tom was no longer a "freedom fighter?" Would they be absolved? Her mind wandered as her cottage came into view. Sean released her hand and ran on ahead. Losing his hand, she abruptly opened her eyes as the sun pierced through the blinds behind the bed, and she watched Sean scrambled away from her, leaving an indent in the mattress where he had cuddled against her all night. They weren't in Lough Tay. They weren't at the cottage. They were here in the safe house in Palmerstown, she realized now with her eyes open. And she had dreamed the same dream two nights in a row. And as she watched her little son anxiously discard his bedclothes and pull on his knee pants and socks, she wiped the sweat from her brow.

She couldn't deny him the excitement of wanting to see his father, although the reality of her surroundings clouded her excitement with anxiety. They needed to get out of the city. Time was not on Tom's side, and she knew it. Thinking clearly now, she recalled that one of Murphy's men had stopped there two nights ago. He was a slovenly chap with little information to share other than blustering about how they'd inflicted monumental damage to the opposition. He did manage to assure her between breathless gulps that Tom and Weasel had escaped and were in a safe house.

That was all she knew so far. She had been advised to stay and wait for him here in Palmerstown. So, last night, she had gathered up Sean and his blanket in the middle of the night and brought him to her bed, where she had spent another restless night between dream and reality, finally succumbing to the fields of Lough Tay in the wee morning hours, only to be assaulted now by the reality of her surroundings.

The boat left that afternoon, and she was beginning to panic. She begrudgingly pulled herself from her bed's warmth and false security and dressed quickly. With a peck on the cheek, Grace instructed Sean to gather up his clothing and place it in the steamer trunk that sat unlatched and expectantly opened by the front door, and she did the same. For the next half an hour, Sean and Grace busied themselves, placing their treasures in the trunk as they had discussed the night before. On top of their clothes and supplies, she carefully placed Nana's lace tablecloth that had been in the family since the thirties. A wedding photo and another of Sean's Christening followed, wrapped carefully in a thick blanket. She constructively made room for the family bible and her copy of James Joyce's "The Importance of Being Ernest" - that was a piece of Ireland she would not abandon. Sean awkwardly cradled a box filled with his best toy trains, his marble collection, and his two favorite books, "Gulliver's Travelers" and "Peter Pan," which Grace carefully squeezed into a spot in the corner of the trunk. Sean felt just like Gulliver and Peter heading out on this new wild adventure to America, and he was busting with excitement.

The night before, Grace had dusted and scrubbed every nook and cranny of the safe house. She wondered why she had spent most of the day cleaning a place that she planned to leave, but it had kept her distracted and had given her closure. This had been like their home. It had kept them close to Tom. It had kept them safe. And now, it's time to move on. She knew not to brood over her husband's activities, or restlessness would certainly prevail, so she had thwarted the nervousness by scrubbing each corner of the little house and each piece of furniture destined to remain. It had also given her a concrete distraction from the barrage of inquiries from her little son. Now that his packing duties were done, Sean was buzzing with excitement, and the barrage resumed.

"Mammy, when are you going to be packed up? Mammy, when will we be leaving? Mammy, have you almost finished the cleaning? "Mammy, when will Daddy be coming back home?" Sean asked Grace for the hundredth time.

The more Grace tried consoling Sean with *"soon,"* the more he pestered her. Her empty promises only aggravated him as the clock ticked on, and he trailed behind her like an unwanted shadow, hindering her housework. A change of tact she thought might settle this child if she was to complete her self-imposed laundry list of chores before her husband's arrival.

"Sean, come on, be a good boy and help me prepare a nice breakfast for Daddy. How about pancakes?"

Grace crouched down to meet Sean's eyes and ran her fingers through his thick, dark mop of hair, an act he disliked but endured for her sake.

"Can I sprinkle the castor sugar Mammy?"

"Of-course you can Sean. Go get the tea" Grace smiled, happy that he was at least momentarily distracted by something else.

The boy set to work prying off the lid on the tin of loose Assam tea-leaves, momentarily lost in the task humming out-of-tune melodies. Grace lifted down the kettle from the shelf to the right of the stove and began to fill it with water from the spigot. "Now we'll wait to heat up the teapot until Daddy gets here, alright. Then, you can scoop in the tea leaves. Why don't you fetch the eggs and milk from the ice box"?

Once the flour, milk, eggs, and butter had all been assembled, Sean demanded wearily, "When will he be here?" "Patience mo mhac," {my son) scolded Grace with a smirk, shaking her finger at him. "Let's get the bowl to make the pancakes…you can help me crack the eggs…what do you say?"

The obedient child carefully retrieved the mixing bowl from the sideboard, placing it gently on the table. As she scooped the butter, she took note of the change in her son's demeanor. Sean was fidgeting with his shirt button and tapping his foot lightly. With the rise and fall of his twitching eyebrows, inquisitive questions raked through his little mind. She knew she was soon to be a victim of his inquisition.

Playfully, he asked in a low and uncertain voice, "Mammy, Daddy is a brave soldier, right? The strongest of them all."

Grace gulped down the lump that had formed in her throat before placing a finger on her lips, urging him not to utter another word. "Sean, how many times have Mammy and Daddy told you not to speak about this? Not to anyone and not out loud as well. It is a secret, one which you are not keeping."

Grace cracked the egg carelessly against the bowl. "Now look what you made me do, Sean... I thought you wanted to help me with the eggs."

She picked the eggshells out of the bowl and then helped Sean crack the next two eggs perfectly in silence. Despite being aware of how much his mother avoided conversing about his father's profession, Sean loved to strum her strings. He had a mind of his own, like his father, and once he was determined to get something, he was relentless.

"Mammy, do you think Daddy would get one of the Black and Tans' big lorries once he shoots them all? Bang, bang, bang," he modelled a gun with his finger and aimed at his mother, shooting the answer right through her. "Three more Tans dead, Mammy, bang bang!"

Sean went around the kitchen with his makeshift gun, taking aim at random objects and pretending to shoot them down. Grace was immobile, half afraid that any passerby would hear him lay claim to the infamous Thomas Sutton and half afraid of how much her son really knew. She reprimanded him swiftly on the bottom with the flat of her hand.

"Sean, you stop right this moment. If you disobey Mammy, then Mammy and Daddy will never tell you a secret again. One day, when you're a big man like your father, you will understand why your Daddy fought. For now, I don't want to hear any more of it, you understand. Now, be a good boy and fetch the mugs from the cupboard while I get this batter finished. I want everything to be ready when Daddy comes back home."

Embarrassed by the smack and the threat of never getting to be the safe keeper of his parents' secrets, Sean mumbled a *'Yes, Mammy'* dejectedly. Grace ruffled Sean's hair once more to his pouting lips, and all was forgiven. They finished the rest of their preparations in silence with an odd mumble here and there. Grace lit the stove and placed the filled kettle to boil, and next to it, methodically melted butter in the pan and ladled in the pancake mixture time and again, flipping and plating, as Sean looked on in silence.

With the pancakes piled and kettle boiled. Grace turned off the stove, rinsed the pan, dried it, and set it aside to cool. Flopping onto the couch, she patted the seat beside her, and Sean scrambled onto the seat next to her, glad to be back in her good graces. Staring out the window at the limitless blue skyline, her tense muscles slowly relaxed, and with that, she began to sob uncontrollably. Sean quickly scooped her wet face in his small hands.

"Why are you crying, Mammy? Is everything alright?"

"Yes, my dear boy. Everything is fine. Which is why I am crying because I am happy today." Grace croaked, taking in the sight of her little boy.

In response, Sean tilted his face to the side and inspected his mother quizzically. "You are crying because you are happy, Mammy? I thought people only cry when they are sad or when something bad happens."

"People cry when they are relieved as well, Sean. This, too, you will understand when you are a big man like Daddy."

"When will I be a big man like him, Mammy?" he said earnestly.

She laughed despite herself, pulling him to her chest. As they chuckled loudly at the silliness. It was a few minutes before Grace noticed the intruder standing within feet of them in the shadow of the doorway. Instinctively, she pulled Sean close to her for safety. She breathed a sigh of relief as she recognized the familiar scrawny outline of their dear old friend. Weasel had slipped in with his key and had been standing at the doorway of the kitchen, stealing this secret moment of warmth and family before him. It was the most tender thing he had seen in weeks, and his soul had been grateful for the stealing.

"You are growing up to be as impulsive as your father, Sean." He mused sincerely.

"Weasel, when did you come in? Where is Thomas?" "Uncle Weasel, where is Daddy?"

"Greetings to you, too, and I am fine. Thank you for asking.

Thomas will be joining us shortly." He laughed playfully.

Rising and bashfully fixing her hair. "I am so sorry. How rude of me, Timothy." Grace embraced him and pecked him on the cheek. She couldn't help but notice the splatters of dried blood on his clothes and the smell of sweat and smoke on his skin. He was a mess.

"Please sit down," Grace said, directing him to the table. "I was just about to make the tea. I have pancakes too… hot off the pan."

"Tea will be fine, thanks," answered Weasel.

"Please let me at least get you a fresh shirt, Tim," she said nervously as she watched Sean's eyes peruse the man's stains. "There is a fresh towel in the bathroom if you want to wash up a little," she said, hopefully pointing in that direction.

"Grand," said Weasel, taking the hint and the shirt with a pained smile. Sean followed him in awe.

How are you holding up?" she called from the kitchen as she poured a small amount of hot water into the teapot to reheat it.

"After crucifying demons? Never felt more alive, Grace." Laughed Weasel from behind the closed door. When he emerged, Sean was already by his side, watching him with wide eyes and an open mouth.

Not wanting Sean to hear all the gory details, she signaled to him with a flick of her wrist and a nod of her head. "You too! Go and wash up, Sean." Sean retreated obediently but looked dejected as Weasel winked mischievously at him.

Grace had heard from the messenger that Weasel's brother had been lost in the fight. She had only met Shamus a few times, but Tom had spoken of him often. Returning now to Weasel with the pot of tea, Grace poured and offered him a tight-lipped smile, unable to find the right words to console him for his loss. She pushed the milk and sugar in his direction.

"So, where is Thomas?"

"What a lucky bastard he is to have such a worrisome and pretty wife, eh? Well, fret not, Grace, your husband is fine. He just needed to make some settlements. He had a hue and cry with Murphy."

"Is everything alright?" worried Grace, turning to face him.

"I suppose, yes. After Murphy picked us up this morning, we went with him to collect the money for our voyage. But after the success of the ambush... he tried coaxing your man to sign on for a couple more against the Black and Tans. That's when our Tom could no longer contain the rage he'd been suppressing since Saturday night, and he pulled that eejit out of his chair by his collar.

"That fecker thought it 'twas child's play to go out there and battle that bloody rogue army." He gulped hard, swallowing back the lump in his throat. "We lost our brothers last night for the betterment of all while he just sat there like a king, with a leg propped on his desk."

"I'm really sorry to hear about your brother, Weasel." Grace finally said. "I don't know what to say, Tim," she uttered apologetically as she reached across the table and rubbed his hand comfortingly.

"He knew what the sacrifice was, Grace. We all did. And now I'll be joining you on your trip to America. It was Tom's idea. I have nothing left here anymore."

"So, you are coming with us, Uncle Weasel? When are we leaving?" piped up Sean as he came out of the bathroom. It was obvious that he had been listening behind the door.

"As soon as your father comes, nosy little gossoon. I hope you Suttons won't mind me presence. Do ya, Sean?" teased Weasel with a chuckle, wiping the tears from his eyes.

"So, what did Tom do, Weasel?" asked Grace, gently trying to get back to the story. She had witnessed Tom's temper before and was afraid for the worst.

"Relax, Grace, he did nothing out of order. He just had to make Murphy see that he was losing his best crew for good. He also owed Tom and me a fair amount, so they had to work out the details and get us off their lists."

"Mammy, can I have the pancakes now?" asked Sean, licking his upper lip.

"Of-course you can Sean," laughed Grace, and she retrieved a dish of pancakes that were warming in the oven. He loved watching the two of them together. It reminded him fondly of his own childhood. Grace was attractive, to be sure, but she also had an uncanny way of warming the hearts of everyone around her with gentle and genuine kindness. When she smiled at you with her piercing sea-green eyes, it was like she had healing powers, he thought.

After she set Sean to sprinkle the castor sugar on the pile of pancakes, Grace poured Weasel another mug of tea, and they sipped tea together and watched Sean impishly lick the sugar off his fingers as if no one was watching.

With her hand over his, she squeezed slightly and, leaning in, she said. "I really am truly sorry about Shamus, Weasel. I know no words can console or compensate you for the loss of your family-especially your brother. I hope you know that we are your family now, always and forever."

Weasel squeezed back as tears welled in his eyes. How lucky Tom was to have found the love of his life. After his second cup of tea and plate of pancakes at Grace's insistence, Weasel's eyes wandered to the black-framed clock on the wall behind the couch.

"Sorry I can't stay longer, Grace, but since I'm leaving with you, I have a bit of packing of me own to attend to, so I'll meet you at the big boat. Murphy may be by to collect you if he feels it's safer for Tom that way. Thanks for breakfast, lass." he said as he wiped the sugar off his lips with the back of his hand and rose from his seat, pulling his cap from his pocket.

"I understand," said Grace

Sean beamed at him through a powdered white beard. "Now, don't you lot be leaving without me?"

"Ha-ha, fret not, Timothy. You are family, remember, and family does not leave each other behind. We will be waiting for you. Either here or at the dock." Grace said emphatically.

Standing now in the doorway, Weasel turned back. "Tis a sad day for the Byrne family when the last one leaves Ireland. My Ma, Da and Shamus are all looking down from the heavens now. I must believe that God left this one lonely Byrne on this earth for a purpose. We shall see!"

Weasel offered them a weak smile, more to console his aching heart than anything else. Sensing his sadness, Sean ran to him, wrapping his arms around his waist. Waving the thoughts of his brother away, he patted Sean's head and pulled the boy into him against his father's oversized shirt.

"Bye, Grace. Bye-bye, Sean." "Bye, Uncle Weasel,"

"Why can you not just call me Uncle Timothy, boy? It does not seem right for a small gossoon like you to call a grown man, Weasel. Don't you think, lad?"

Sean caught on to the teasing and rendered some of his own Weasel's way, "As you wish, Uncle Weasel!"

"You're a cheeky boy! You may look like your Mammy, but you're just like your father, impulsive and stubborn. Can't I even ask my little godson to call me Uncle Timothy, Grace? Weasel teased.

"Alright, fine, I give in…Weasel it is!" Weasel conceded without a fight.

Grace had to laugh. Weasel had succeeded in lifting all their moods. And with a wink and tip of his cap, he bid them adieu. Once he was out of sight, she locked the door behind him and retreated to the kitchen to wait for Tom.

Weasel was careful to check the street. Everything was clear from top to bottom. With expediency, Weasel barreled down the street heading towards the main road, his hat pulled down low over his eyes and Tom's shirt floating in the wind behind him like a short dress. He had several loose strings to tie up in a very short time. As he rounded the corner, his chest nearly imploded like someone had kicked the air out of him. A mere sixty feet away, moving in his direction, was a lorry full of Black and Tans. He instantly recognized Smith and the Corporal, one of the worst of them, turned tail and began running in the opposite direction.

"Look, it's that Weasel," exclaimed Smith to the Sergeant. "Weasel?" Armstrong questioned in his thick Scottish accent.

"Timothy Byrne, Sir. He goes by the name of Weasel. The fastest man in Ireland. He was one of the assailants from last night. He's

Sutton's right-hand man." explained Smith with venom dripping from his tongue.

"Over there, Sir, look, he's running down that alley."

"Stop the truck right here. Five of you come with me to catch this, Timothy Byrne. Corporal, you, and Smith watch Sutton's house. Just watch…nobody enters in my absence. understood?"

As the truck came to a halt, Armstrong jumped off with five men in tow and waited for a response to his orders before taking chase after Weasel. He knew he would have to answer to the major if anything nefarious went down with Sutton's capture. The corporal gave a lethargic and curt response, unfazed by the sergeant's authority. *"Yes, Sergeant. Right Smith?"* he said lazily. Smith nodded. Satisfied, Armstrong yelled at his foot soldiers, and they took off after Weasel.

Weasel was nimble and had been known to effectively evade the authorities before. He ran breathlessly, taking only a second here and there to mark his distance from his pursuers. Running right past Sutton's home, he prayed deliberately, *"Dear God, please protect Grace and Sean from these wicked bastards. Jaysus, where are you, Thomas? Your family is in grave danger, man!"* He wanted to cry out and warn Grace, but he knew it was best to keep their location secret. He wasn't sure if the British had uncovered the address or if they were just patrolling Palmerstown.

He surmised that his skinny legs had covered nearly a distance of two miles by now, but they were still in pursuit. He knew it would be a death sentence if he was caught. So, he had to make the offi-cer in charge give up chasing him and return to his command. Up ahead, Weasel spotted a run-down cottage set back off the road a bit. Before barging through the front door, he let his presence be known in Gaelic to the occupant. A heavyset old woman donning a fresh head of curlers, housecoat, and slippers emerged at the door. Despite the unusual circumstances, the stranger seemed more than willing and perhaps even a bit excited to help her fellow countryman. She promptly let him in, closed the door behind her, and ushered him quickly out the small back window, like she knew what to do.

There, as promised, he found leaning against the gate, a rusty old bicycle in all its grandeur. This mode of transportation, which had clearly carried a hefty man around Dublin in better days, was now his best and only escape plan. He tipped his cap to the old woman, who offered him a reassuring gaze, and he climbed aboard the fragile frame and took off down the alley behind her house.

This was now his only means of saving Grace and Sean from the Black and Tans. They were close, and he didn't want to imagine the outcome if they didn't get out soon. His thoughts were only interrupted by the sounds of bullets ricocheting off the old woman's gate posts as two robust men took aim at him from the minute window, which had clearly been too small for them to squeeze through. He had the distance now, and their shots were futile.

Eyeing the Scotsman in his big boots standing in the middle of her living room, the old woman bellowed, "This is not the Amiens Street Station, but my cottage you're standing in, young man!"

The wrinkles on the woman's forehead were more prominent now, running deep like furrows in a potato field, and she glared with none of the warmth she had shown Weasel. "First, some eejit barges through me door and steals me boy's bicycle. Now you British rogues are rummaging through me property. I've heard nasty things about them, Black and Tans. Dare lay a hand on me and my virtue, and I'll scream till I'm black and blue."

Armstrong realized they had gone too far, busting through her door, and quickly retreated, nodding to his men and removing his hat to offer her a small bow of apology.

"Don't you worry, madam; we will harm you. I am an officer of the British Army."

"I'm no eejit, mister. I took note of how you don't wear the wee black beret of the Black and Tans like the rest of those braggarts. But just the same, I want you out of my house right this minute. I am worried for me life with your mere presence. Lord knows what monstrosity those braggarts will inflict on me," She spoke in a trembling voice and pulled her house coat tightly around her. As she employed every dramatic bone in her body, she motioned to the men who stood staring at her from the window,

"Pardon us, madam, for intruding. We will leave this very instant," repeated Armstrong as he swiftly ushered the men out of the small cottage, nodding again upon their exit in apology.

Scowling angrily, the old woman watched in satisfaction as all the braggarts, in their army boots, bowed before her upon their exit, trying to avoid hitting their heads against the low doorframe. Once they were out, she slammed the door loudly to punctuate that the British army was not welcome in her abode.

"He got away this time too, sergeant."

"Thank you for pointing out the obvious," sneered Armstrong, panting. "How far are we from Sutton's place?" That had to have been where he was coming from?"

"Maybe three miles from here, Sir?"

"Slow march back there, then." sighed Armstrong, recognizing that he might have been able to outrun a man like Weasel in his youth. Was he getting old, or did Weasel actually live up to his name-sake, "The fastest man in Ireland?"

Outside the Sutton residence, they had been sitting in the truck with the engine off. Smith had been trying to persuade his corporal to abandon his orders. It had only been ten minutes, but he was already impatient.

"I'm telling you, corporal, there is no point in waiting for them to return. Weasel could have them occupied for hours on end. Remember how he made us run around and around in circles a couple of months ago. There is no chance of them catching him anytime soon."

"Orders are orders, Smith," the corporal replied, "even if I don't like them. We will have our chance." He said as he absentmindedly sipped on the whiskey bottle in his hand.

Smith continued, "To hell with the orders, corporal. Think of this: if we get Sutton before the sergeant arrives, then you'll probably be promoted to sergeant yourself."

The two men bantered back and forth, exchanging the bottle of whiskey between them. When the contents were fully imbibed, and intoxication had settled in nicely, the corporal surveyed the street. At least 30 minutes had now passed, and there was no sign of the other men.

"You know what, Mr. Smith, perhaps you are right. The orders can go to hell. I'd be a better sergeant than that Scottish fool anyway."

"That's what a sergeant should sound like, confident of himself." Smith flattered him with a mock salute.

Slurring their words, they swung open the truck door and slid off the seat onto the street below, slamming the door behind them and tossing the empty bottle to the curb. Sutton's house stood before them, waiting.

CHAPTER 6

Part 2: Leaving Home

In front of the door, Smith patted Corporal Jensen on his shoulder encouragingly. They both swayed slightly with inebriation as the corporal cleared his throat. "Sutton, this is the British army here for your arrest. Come out now."

On the other side of the door, Grace's eyes shifted like a scared mouse from the door to Sean, who sat at the table staring back at her, a mouthful of pancakes bulging through his pursed lips. She made an SHH sign with her finger. Her heart was racing. How had the British found the safe house? And with an arrest warrant so fast? Who would have betrayed this address to the British? That was considered the lowest form of treachery.

There was nowhere to escape to, and she was sure they had the house surrounded anyway. They would never hurt a woman and a child, she reassured herself. Maybe it was best that Tom hadn't made it back to the safe house. Even if they took her in for questioning, she had done nothing wrong and really had no details of Tom's exploits. They had always kept it that way. She touched the cross around her neck, the one Tom had given her when Sean was born, and prayed to God to keep Tom safe. Maybe Weasel had intercepted him and warned him to stay away. She just needed to stand her ground and send them on their way.

On the door's front side, the corporal shrugged, and the two men grimaced at each other. This time, Smith took the lead and rapped loudly, commanding, "Sutton, we are here for your arrest. Come out immediately."

A woman's voice responded low and clearly laced with fear. "My husband is not at home. Only my son and I are here."

Snickering, the corporal whispered to his subordinate, "Well, I'll be dammed Smith if it's not Sutton's old lady."

This time, he yelled loudly with a sneer, "Oh, come on out already, Sutton. Haven't you had enough sheltering under your missus' skirt?"

Grace peeked carefully through the blind and saw that the men's uniforms were not those of the British Army, but they were Black and Tans. Grace's fear escalated as she backed into the kitchen, holding Sean close to her, trying to put as much distance as possible between her and the Black and Tans. She yelled again. "He's not here…I don't know where he is. Please just leave my lad and me alone."

She knew from the stories that these men lacked any real allegiance to a code of military conduct, and she felt her situation was becoming more fragile by the second. She had to somehow make them believe she was alone, and this was a moot manhunt. She pulled Sean in, and the little boy snaked his arms around his mother's waist for protection.

Grace tried to mask her fear by sounding more resolute this time, and she answered the corporal once more, "Sir, he is not here."

"Stop lying and send your man out." insisted Smith

"I am not lying to you. Thomas is not home, and I don't know where he is." Grace stated with finality and truthfulness.

"We don't believe you. Prove your words are true and let Sutton Jr. open the door then, eh. We promise we will do no harm to your child."

"Then, will you leave us alone?" Grace uttered with trepidation. "You have my word," Corporal Jensen answered in a flat tone while Smith muffled a snicker at her expense.

She had to get rid of them and quickly. Uncurling her son from her waist, she crouched down to face him, and his eyes met hers knowingly. Grace gently placed her hand on Sean's shoulder blade, instructing him to be brave. Sean returned her gaze with pure fear. Whispering in his ear, she assured him that he had no reason to be afraid because he was the son of the courageous Thomas Edward Sutton. All he had to do was tell the truth…his father was not home, and he didn't know where he was. And then the bad men would leave.

Protruding his chest, Sean unlatched the door and opened it halfway, slipping out in front of the threshold. Mustering all the courage he could, he put his hands on his hips, looked them dead in the eyes, and said, *"My Da's not home. Don't know where he is. Now go away."*

The two men broke down in hysterics like two drunkards at a pub looking for a fight. Once the men gathered themselves, Smith surveyed Sean from head to foot. He Pulled his rifle strap off his shoulder and raised the weapon, slowly pointing it at Sean's head. "You know, corporal, he's going to grow just like his fava and shoot men like us. I should just make things easy for us and put him out of his misery now."

Grace screamed, "NO!" as she pulled open the door to rescue her boy.

The corporal knocked back the rifle and pulled Smith away from the door. As Sean stood on the threshold, a wet patch grew and ran down one side of his pants onto his stocking feet. The corporal may have been under the influence of the drink, too, but was well aware that their actions would be documented. If they killed a child, they would be arrested and would face a military tribunal. Sean retreated from the puddle on the doorstep and embarrassedly slipped back into the house into Grace's arms, slamming the door behind him.

"Be careful, Smith," he said with a smile. "You just can't go and kill the boy. He's already pissed his pants. You're a tosser. That's one for Sutton's legacy, alright."

Laughing, Corporal Jensen patted Smith on the shoulder, demonstrating his solidarity. "Now, let's go have a word with Sutton's old lady, shall we? She's a sweet thing?

"I'll tell you if he had been home, Sutton would never have let his child open the door to us, that's clear. She's scared shitless and will squeal for sure. Isn't what we came here for, right?" Smith nodded with a smirk.

Approaching the door again, this time, they didn't wait for an invitation but turned the knob and swung the door wide open. As the men stumbled over the threshold into the front hallway, Sean watched them falter, stumbling over their own boots. He had seen grown men act like this before, and he had smelled the reek of alcohol coming from them in the doorway. He remembered his father had warned him of the drink and what it could do to men- Da, always avoided Murphy when he'd been drinking, he remembered. He always got cross easily and cursed a lot. It made Sean uneasy.

Despite his insobriety, the corporal didn't fail to notice the nearly packed trunk agape against the wall. Grace clung to Sean several feet away, ruffling his hair absentmindedly and assuring him everything would be fine. The corporal and Private Smith were on the other end of the living room when their eyes landed on Grace and Sean huddled on the couch.

A sly, lopsided grin broke out on Smith's face, and the corporal spoke in a slick, businesslike tone, "So, you are Sutton's old lady?"

"From my view, she is not all that old, corporal," Smith smirked, making Grace stand and absentmindedly correct her yellow cotton day dress, which hugged her delicate figure.

Grace knew that she must be a stalwart. She told herself They only wanted Tom, and she honestly had no information about his current whereabouts. She was no Cumann na mBan activist, but she was aware of the brutal hair shorning with blunt blades or scissors perpetrated on women. Sometimes, they ripped the hair out by the roots. This behavior, along with brutal rapes inflicted on Irish females by the British army's hired hands, was condemned most everywhere. Be strong and confident, Grace. Look them in the eyes, and don't elaborate.

She lifted her face and spoke with newfound confidence. "I am Mrs. Sutton. You have not been true to your word despite my telling you the truth, and you have frightened my lad. Like I told you before, my husband is not here."

"I gave my word not to harm your son, and I stand firm on that." assured the corporal, attempting to be the voice of authority as he looked at the boy's soiled pants with a smirk.

Grace squeezed Sean tighter as he sobbed pitifully into her dress. "Now, is this any way to treat fine gentlemen like us wif such an 'ostile manner, Mrs. Sutton? We just came 'ere for your husband. I see you are planning a trip, a long one by the sight of the trunk in the 'allway. So now you must know his whereabouts?" Both folded their hands, facing her in a stand-off. Smith gave Grace a slow and unsettling once over.

Looking at her feet, trying to avoid Smith's menacing gaze, Grace said slowly and emphatically, "I really don't know where he is."

Not wanting to miss out on the fun, the corporal joined in. "Well, now, we don't wish to trouble your pretty head, now do we, darling?

"Why don't we make this easy for you? Stop lying and give us your husband's whereabouts, and we will leave. If you don't, we will remain here and wait for him in your good company." Smith said with undertones that Grace absorbed with every fiber of her being.

Fighting the urge to cry, Grace released Sean, folded her arms in front of her, and, pinching her elbow hard for moral courage, stepped forward and shouted defiantly. "I don't know where he is, and that's God's honest truth. I already told you that. Now please leave."

In response, the corporal quickly stepped towards her and slapped her swiftly across her face, leaving a vivid red mark on her creamy cheek. Anger rose like a torrent in Sean, and he charged at the corporal, hurling kicks and punches at him in a fury. The corporal lifted Sean by the collar of his shirt in mid-air as Grace rushed to him, screaming, 'No, Sean. Stop…don't hurt him, please don't hurt him."

Smith grabbed Grace's shoulder hard and held her back. The corporal carried the boy, now gasping for air, to the bedroom and threw him roughly on the bed. Looking down at Sean, small and whimpering on the bed, he grinned sanctimoniously. "Now that's how we discipline a baby coward that pisses his pants, alright son... tell your father that?"

"That's how it's done, Smith-you see grinned the corporal emerging from the room. "Just a little discipline...that's all that's required."

Grace heard Sean's heaving sobs from the other room and ran at the corporal as Smith closed in behind her. She scratched and punched viciously at Corporal Jensen and then at Smith, who just laughed at her useless attempts while hot, angry tears rolled down her cheeks. She received another blow to her chin, only this time it was Smith, and the force of the impact made her stumble backwards and fall. Smith spat mockingly in her direction. She crawled herself into a standing position and made a dash for the bedroom. The men just laughed as she rushed to bolt the door behind her.

Grace curled herself on the bed, embracing Sean tightly in the hopes of absorbing his sobs and his trauma. Her jaw ached where the last blow had landed, but she smiled at him and ran her fingers through his hair. Rocking him in her arms, she sang softly, "Sleep, my child, for the red bee hums. The silent twilight falls."

Loud thuds echoed throughout the house as the table and chairs were overturned.

"Eivell from the grey rock comes. To wrap the world in thralls." she continued, voice shaking.

Her china cups hit the ground and shattered, and the kettle struck the wall.

"And lyin' there, oh, my child, my joy. My love and heart's desire." She continued. Grace prayed that Tom had a plan to get them out. Did he even know they were here? For the first time, she feared for their survival.

On the other side of the cottage, alcohol now permeated the veins of the two men wrecking Sutton's kitchen. They laughed and cursed loudly, proud of their destruction and the power they had wielded upon their infamous enemy. Finding another half, a bottle of whiskey in the kitchen cabinet, they passed and shared gulps, mocking toasts to Thomas' health, his missus, and his courageous lad as whiskey dripped down their chins like drool.

Now slurring his words, Smith proposed, "Why are we wasting our time out here when we are in the company of an attractive woman, Corp?"

"Arrgh. She'll only scream like a banshee and alert the neighbors like the bitch she is. Plus, it was the Scotsman's orders not to lay a hand on them."

"No, he said not to enter. Smith clarified. And we are in here already, right? If you know what I mean, Corp, we won't need to lay our hands on her. Think of it…come on. We will be awake and alert when that bastard Sutton returns, and what an injury to his manhood, don't you think…to have a piece of his little whore. Plus, I know just the way to shut her mouth."

The corporal couldn't contain his excitement. Was it revenge or the liquor talking? He couldn't tell, but he didn't care. He was ready, and she'd be willing. "Why didn't you say so, Smith?"

Grace had heard every word. If they got through that door, she had only one objective: to protect Sean at all costs and to prevent him from seeing what she knew would be inevitable. She pushed a heavy wooden chair quickly against the door to brace it. But it was no use. With one swift kick with his army boot, the door came off the hinge. Grace screamed, backing into the corner of the room with Sean behind her, as Smith and Jensen approached, discarding the chair easily as they entered.

Smith was now armed with his backup weapon, a revolver, and a deadly look of hunger in his beady black eyes. He took excruciatingly slow steps toward Grace, intimidating her into submission as she sheltered Sean behind her. She wanted to get Sean to hide under the bed, away from this impending scene, but she was frozen by the barrel of his gun, unsure of his state of mind or willingness to kill them.

The corporal stood at the entrance of the now broken door. Watching his subordinate overpower her made his hunger more voracious by the second. Smith pulled Sean out from behind Grace with his weaponless hand, never losing eye contact with her. Sean struggled to hold onto her dress, which ripped as Smith pulled him free.

Now, moving the revolver to Sean's temple, he leaned in close to Grace, reeking of liquor. "We'll make you another deal. Your husband apparently is not bothered about your safety. Darling, let us be clear: we'd enjoy taking him down in cold blood as soon as he crosses that doorstep, but we have our orders to take him alive. So, while we wait, we thought it would be courteous of you to serve my friend and me what we want? "That's the least Thomas Sutton's whore could do for us, and in return, you and your boy get to live."

Smith licked his lips while keeping full eye contact with Grace. Grace understood, and her beautiful green eyes filled with tears. She fell on her knees with her hands clasped and begged for them to leave her and Sean alone. As Sean, witnessing his mother begging for their lives, struggled free from Smith's grip and screamed with the high-pitched shriek of a child, gripped onto his mother. Smith took the back of his revolver and struck Sean against the head, knocking him down with one blow. He fell like a sack of potatoes, limp and lifeless. Grace screamed in desperation and reached out to Sean on the floor, tugging at his motionless little feet. She pleaded once more. "Please, leave us alone. What wrong have we done to you?" "He is just an innocent child."

The Corporal now interjected, walking towards Sean's motionless body. "Now, Sutton's missus, your boy isn't dead yet. If you want him to live, then just do as my man here says. Place yourself here on the bed, and we will take care of the rest. She looked up at him in fear.

"You either do as I say, or I tie you to the bed, and we will do to you as we please, then I'll let Smith here empty his revolver into your child's head?"

Grace knew she had lost. There was no way out of this now. Please, God, Sean was still alive...at least he wouldn't have a memory of what was about to befall his mother. She could never face him after that. She was just a body, she told herself, nothing more. This meant nothing. These men were drunk. They'd do their business and then leave her and Sean alone. Tom would arrive and carry them off to America. She could do this. She got up off the floor. Without emotion, she closed her eyes and heaved a sigh. She reopened her eyes with no emotion and requested Smith lay her boy's head on a pillow. She demanded that they confirm her boy was fine, and then she would do whatever they said without resisting.

Happy not to hear any more screaming or crying, they placed Sean's head on a pillow in the corner of the room and confirmed he was breathing. She then crossed herself - this was between herself and God. She methodically unbuttoned her sunny yellow dress and let it fall to the floor. Both men were ready, but Smith bowed to his corporal, indicating that he could go first.

Grace crossed to the corporal in compliance, emotionless. He couldn't contain his lust anymore and ripped her chemise off her shoulder, revealing her breast. He pulled down the other side and began to grope and feast on her breasts like an animal. It didn't care that he punctured her skin with his teeth, and a trickle of blood ran down from her left nipple, staining her white petticoat. Digging his teeth and nails into her skin, he threw her roughly on the bed. Grace clenched her eyes shut and, kept her compass on Sean and Tom and prayed for strength. With grunts full of hot, stale whisky, he hitched himself forcefully into her. She wept silently, apologizing to Tom for allowing this animal to take what was only meant for him. The mattress was moist with tears. Finally, exhausted, the beast of a man heaved himself off her abused body and rolled off the bed laughing.

Smith's belt was already off, and he was unzipped. He wasted no time, however, to remove any clothing but pressed down heavily on Grace. He was even rougher than the corporal claiming her again and again, unbothered by his trousers still being on. The corporal barely guarded the boy, being too entertained by the sight of Smith devouring the piece of skin where his own mouth was moments before as he watched drunkenly from the floor. Grace stared at the ceiling. She pretended that her heart and soul were disconnected from her body. He saw the cottage on Lough Tay and Sean's mop of hair bouncing as he ran down the hill to meet his father. She saw Tom's face, his beautiful face, and his hands tenderly stroking the hair from her face. His other hand held hers around a metal object…he was talking to her. He was showing her something. It was a revolver. He was showing her how to aim it…she was laughing. She looked to the right, and there on the bed next to her lay Smith's revolver. He had relinquished it in his fervor, throwing it on the bed beside her. His panting was beginning to slow; he was nearly spent, and his revolver was within reach.

The corporal couldn't see her stealthy maneuver from the floor on the other side of the bed when she gripped the handle and found the trigger. In one swift motion, she raised the weapon and pulled the trigger. Almost instantly, the bed sheet beneath her was soaked in crimson. Smith fell limp against her, his blood spilling onto her. The corporal looked around in horror, momentarily unaware of what had happened, reaching for his discarded clothing frantically.

Moving quickly, Grace pushed Smith aside and took aim at the corporal. He was trouser-less and weaponless. She fired, hitting him in the shoulder and then again. This time the blast was loud and bloody, but her aim was accurate right to the head, just like Tom had taught her, and his body collapsed on the ground in a lifeless heap. For one grand moment, Grace stood triumphantly. She had defended her honor and saved her son. But the gunfire and shouting had brought back the British troops. Busting through the door, they fired rounds of bullets wildly.

Grace watched in horror as a stray bullet hit Sean. His little body flinched and then stillness. And just as easily, another found her heart. Half-naked and broken, she fell back motionless onto blood and down feathers. When the assault came to an end, Sergeant Armstrong entered to survey the horrifying sight before them.

Assessing the bedroom scene, Armstrong first noticed the lifeless body of a small boy in the corner of the room and then the corpse of a young woman, which one of his men had discreetly covered with a yellow garment he had found on the floor. He quickly ordered his men to remove Smith and Jensen's bodies from her side.

"Dear God, what have these pigs done? Get these pigs out of my sight NOW!"

Two soldiers moved the bloodied, half-naked bodies of Smith and Jensen into the living room.

He had to get air. He feared he couldn't catch a breath in this place. And stepping back outside the cottage, he ordered one of the soldiers to call in Major Siddley immediately. He did not want to be the one to tackle this mess. These were innocents, a woman, and a child, for God's sake. He thought of his own wife and children and had to force back the lump in his throat. Sutton was no friend of theirs, but this carnage was unspeakable. Regaining his composure, Sergeant Armstrong reentered the house and moved into the bedroom. He carefully removed the sunny yellow dress that had been partially draped over Grace and forced himself to take in the monstrosity before him, almost as penance. In one ghastly image, he understood what had occurred and how this had ended. He paced his breathing and reverently took off his overcoat, placed it over her body, and crossed himself.

Standing again on the threshold, breathing in the fresh air, Sergeant Armstrong wondered at the questions that would arise from his superiors. Like Major Siddley, he had never approved of these so-called Black and Tans. This was not the way the British Army did things and certainly not how he had been trained.

When it was discovered that she had been violently raped and the child killed, there would be hell to pay. Aside from the authorities, what kind of havoc would a man wreak, who has lost his wife and child, especially like this. He, for one, would want blood, he decided. Regardless of how much of a criminal Thomas Sutton was, his wife and lad were innocent and did not deserve to meet their ends this way.

His ruminations dissipated as one of the soldiers called out from within the house. *"The boy is alive, sir. He has a pulse."*

Armstrong rushed to the boy's side. Please, God, let him save the child, he thought. Crouching next to the boy, he saw the damage and quickly pulled off and then fastened his belt above Sean's knee. He then rushed to find something clean to bind it with from the dresser. Returning with a clean folded sheet, he ripped off a strip and wrapped it tightly around the wound on the boy's leg. Sean was mumbling incoherently. Armstrong stroked the boy's head, as he would with his own child, and told him he was alright and to rest.

All Sean could say was, "Mammy. Mammy, Mammy." The soldier who had found Sean's pulse was ordered to sit with the child until a doctor could be called.

"Pray for the child and for all our sins to be pardoned, soldier. The immoral actions of our men bring shame upon us all," said Armstrong meaningfully. The soldier nodded in agreement.

Hearing the distinctive sound of his Morris Cowley screeching to a halt outside, Armstrong made his way to the front door to greet Major Siddley. Before entering the crime scene, his authoritative voice bellowed outside from the road, demanding an explanation of what had happened. Sergeant Armstrong met him outside and bowed his head in respect. Before launching into any explanation, he ushered forward the soldier who still cradled Sean in his arms, explaining that the boy was still alive and that they were waiting for the doctor.

The Major immediately insisted they forgo the doctor and have his driver transport the boy immediately to Royal City Hospital in his car. With a wave to his driver, the soldier who had attended to him carried Sean to the major's car. Carefully nestling Sean's unconscious head on his lap, Armstrong and Siddley watched the car door slam and sped away.

Once inside, the major surveyed the demolition. Overturned furniture lay motionless amidst broken glass and crockery. Proceeding to the bedroom, he stopped beside the bed laden with Grace's veiled corpse. He moved to lift the overcoat when Sergeant Armstrong gently tapped his shoulder, nodding in disdain. "The sight is of utmost horror, Sir. She was a beautiful young woman, sir, who lost her life tragically for no reason. It is truly a disgrace for us."

What in the hell happened here, sergeant?" Major Siddley demanded

When my men and I arrived here, Weasel, his partner, was spotted running down the street. We assumed he had just left this location and Sutton himself."

"Go on," said Siddley patiently.

"So, I ordered Corporal Jensen and Private Smith to guard Sutton's house in case he was inside or in the event he attempted to return. Strict orders, I assure you, were given to not enter his domicile, and they understood he was to be apprehended alive. I then took the other men, and we went after Weasel. I expected that we would catch the man and return shortly thereafter. However, they disobeyed my orders in my absence and entered the home. Upon returning, we heard shots fired from inside, and my men dashed in. We assumed that the corporal and private were being attacked, and in the retaliatory fire, Mrs. Sutton and her boy were shot." He hung his head and sighed deeply.

"Do you deem the results of the retaliatory fire an accident, sergeant?"

"Yes, Sir. My men were unaware of the brutality inflicted by Corporal Jenkins and Private Smith. Based on the gunshots heard from the street, they were deployed only in defense. It appears that Mrs. Sutton shot Smith and Jensen since Smith's revolver was discovered in her grip. Lowering his voice now, "Everything indicates that both men violated Sutton's wife."

Breathing a deep sigh, Siddley smiled sadly at the sergeant. "Thank you for saving me the horror of looking at her body. This must be the worst thing I have seen in my career. I, for one, am glad she had some vengeance before she died. I found both those men disdainful. May she rest in peace."

Moving into the living room with Armstrong by his side, he addressed the remaining men. "I am deeply disturbed by what has occurred here today. This is not the way the British Army conducts itself. We will all need to atone for the sins of these men. Turning to Armstrong, he stated emphatically, "I will take care of the boy personally."

"What about the bodies, Sir?" said one of the soldiers

"Take Mrs. Sutton to the morgue, then lock the house, and leave two men behind to guard it. Later, send the truck back to pick up the bodies of those worthless bastards."

"Can't they all be accommodated within one truck Sir?" said a private, who was standing over the bodies of Smith and Jensen.

"No, they cannot! I shall not disgrace this woman further. Separately understand!" They all nodded their heads in understanding.

Armstrong lifted Grace, still covered in his overcoat. He noted the open steamer trunk in the hallway as he carried her over the threshold into the sunshine. This would be her final farewell to her little safe house, which had proved to be the opposite. Neighbors had now emerged from their houses as Grace's body was laid in the truck stationed outside. Her funeral serenade was a cacophony of hurled profanities and wailing from strangers full of resentment and loathing. They barely knew the young woman, but they mourned her death, they mourned for the innocent, and they mourned for Ireland.

Siddley knew that it was not Sutton who was a hero for the cause, but his wife Grace who had become a martyr for it. The crowd dispersed as the army vehicle growled its way towards the city, leaving behind a trail of whispers that would echo for decades to come.

CHAPTER 7

The British Major

Weasel threw the dilapidated bike against the brick wall and raced up the back stairs to Murphy's room. Breathless and wringing with sweat, he instantly barraged Murphy with questions about Tom's whereabouts, looking frantically around the room.

Murphy shrugged absentmindedly. "What do you mean where is he? He just left here as we planned. Don't you remember Weasel? He was very to the point, if you know what I mean" Murphy rubbed his bruised chin awkwardly.

Weasel ploughed forward madly. "Oh God, how far could he have walked by now?" Do you think we can stop him in time?

"Listen, we've had an ear to the ground in Palmerstown since Sunday. It's been quiet. As soon as I got you both out, I told the watch to take a break. Figured Tom was here with me anyway. Weasel, what the hell is going on?"

Now, he was making eye contact and slowing his speech so that Murphy would get the message loud and clear "Something horrible has happened, Murphy. We need to stop Tom before he gets to Palmerstown. He stared at Murphy intently, like a madman, and choked, "They have killed Grace and Sean."

Covering his eyes with the palm of his hand, he heaved a deep sob, and the caged tears he had kept suppressed during this jaunt through the streets of Dublin now escaped freely. Murphy watched the man dissolve before him while he stood silent and in shock. Then like a lit match, he sprang into action, pulling Weasel almost off his feet and dragging him down the stairs to the back door where his car, covered with a tarp, waited in the alley.

"We have to get to him… we need to stop him before he finds out," Murphy said, ripping the tarp of his car, which he kept hidden in the alley. He deliberately pushed Weasel towards the passenger side and aggressively flung the driver's side door open. *"Get in, man!"* he ordered. Weasel clambered inside.

"How did it happen, Weasel?" Murphy asked without looking up at Weasel as he pulled the car out.

"I only heard that their bodies were taken away in one of their trucks."

"Was Grace…?" Weasel only looked away, wiping a tear from his cheek. That was the answer enough. Murphy knew what the Black and Tans were capable of. Silence overcame them like a prayer of sorts as they drove on in silence.

Murphy should have insisted that he drive Tom to Palmerstown, but his ego and chin had been bruised after he tried to rope Tom and Weasel into another series of ambushes by withholding their money. He had met with the full extent of Tom's rage and had a throbbing jaw to prove it. Now he realized just how insensitive he had been. The man had just lost some of his best mates, had made promises to his wife that he had vowed to keep, and his own life was in danger. But all Murphy could think about was losing a huge asset to the organization, especially after the success of the recent ambush. So regretfully, when Tom said he'd walk instead, Murphy didn't stop him.

Tom had left Murphy's place in a clean suit and dress shoes, not his typical wardrobe. He had slicked back his hair and even replaced his flat cap with a fedora. He looked more like a genteel man about town than an insurrectionist. He was keenly aware that the British were after him, so he had decided months before that he would need to change his outward appearance for this journey. Before heading to Palmerstown, he wanted to take one last walk through Dublin. This town was his literal blood brother. In it, he had felt immense loyalty and tragic loss. His reward, a stack of two hundred pounds, was tucked away safely inside his suit coat pocket, along with Weasel's reward. He felt euphoric and yet somehow melancholic for this familiarity he was about to lose. He was no longer a freedom fighter.

He tried to adsorb his surroundings. The smell wafting from McFardle's fish and chip stand mingled with voices in Gaelic as he passed by. He may never hear and smell those two things together again, he thought. He pulled his scarf around the bottom of his face and brought his hat down to brush his eyebrows. He realized the car ride would have been a safer choice, but he felt like he had earned this final walk-through of Dublin's fair city. Grace would understand. He had to breathe in his Ireland one last time. These images would become memories for his mind's eye when he felt nostalgic.

When he was a boy, this had been a more peaceful town than the whole country had been, but this year alone had seen some of the worst bloodshed to date. As he crossed Talbot Street to O'Connell Street before heading towards Kingsbridge via the Quay, he looked out over the Quay and thought back to the dockside workers' boycott earlier in the Spring. A fervor had spread through Dublin then.

Looking out over the river, he paused for a moment in respect for his departed comrades. They had given their lives for this land, and they would forever inhabit it. Everything had accelerated after the murder of Tomás Mac Curtain, Sinn Féin's Lord Mayor of Cork, who was murdered in his home by British crown forces on 20 March 1920. Soon after their murders, they saw the infiltration of the Black and Tans.

Since March, it had been one insurrection after another, culminating in the sacking of Balbriggan in Fingal. So, who knew in what direction this fight for freedom was headed? Or maybe he had just lost his faith in the cause altogether. His allegiance to it had deprived them of a normal life. His heart skipped with excitement, thinking of a new life in America. It was time… and he was ready. Tomorrow was a new beginning.

He was brought out of his trance by the banter of a young audience who had gathered to gawk at the wrecked vehicles on the other side of the river on Aston Quay. The haunting ground where the remains of broken bodies of men had been dragged from the Liffey, which now concealed Flynn's final resting place.

"This is no place for paisti. Go home," Tom ordered in Gaelic with authority as the children scurried away from the war zone. How many of these youngsters someday would be caught in the fray, he wondered? Thank God for his son never would. He quickened his pace towards Palmerstown.

About a mile from his house, they spotted him. Weasel leaned out the window, shouting erratically, as the car screeched to a halt. Now face to face, Weasel shouted at Tom, "Get in the damn car, Tom."

"Why are you here…and Murphy? Is everything alright?" said Tom, stopping dead in his tracks, sensing something had gone array.

"Just get in the damn car, Sutton. I don't have time to explain.

Get in the car now!" Murphy said nervously but with authority.

Sensing the danger, Tom did as he was demanded and climbed into the back seat. As soon as the car door slammed, Murphy took off with a vengeance.

"Did something happen? What the hell is going on? Will someone answer me, God Damnit?"

Without looking at him, Weasel stared straight ahead and whispered in a low voice. "Thomas, your house was raided by the Tans a couple of hours ago,"

"What about Grace and Sean? Where are they? You got them out, didn't you?" Tom said feverishly. No response.

"What about Grace and Sean…Murphy? Weasel…are they alright?"

Tom was breathing heavily now. Weasel's lips trembled with grief. This time, he turned in his seat to face Tom. No words were necessary. Tom could see it in Weasel's eyes as they filled with tears.

"They have been killed, Thomas," Weasel said in a barely audible whisper.

Stunned, Tom retreated into the seat and stared blankly at Weasel. Blood drained from his face as both men stared at him through the car's rearview mirror. Murphy and Weasel brushed away tears, and then from the deep cavernous well of fury, Tom screamed out at the top of his lungs, a deafening wail that turned pedestrian heads and shocked horses and passengers alike in their tracks as they drove past. His pain turned quickly to anger, and he reeled around and punched his fist through the car window. He was manic.

The shattering glass drove Murphy to jolt the car to a stop. As soon as the car stopped, Tom flung open the car door and took off in the opposite direction, back towards Palmerstown. *This couldn't be true…maybe he wasn't too late. He could save them, he thought. He just had to get back there…they needed him.* He rationalized his own reality as he sprinted without care for his own safety. Murphy wasted no time but put his sedan into reverse, ripping off the spare tire as he collided with the wall near Phoenix Park. They were again in pursuit with all the gusto his engine could muster.

As the vehicle neared their target, Weasel opened the door, and half-balancing on the running board, he let go and jumped onto Tom, bringing him to the ground. As the men wrestled on the cracked pavement, Murphy screeched the car to a halt and, exiting, rounded the car to join them. Onlookers had begun to take notice of the kerfuffle now, and windows and doors creaked open to take in the scene unfolding on the street before them. Tom lashed out at Weasel, landing a punch clearly on his chin, pummeling him backwards, as Murphy, a much smaller man than Tom, went for Tom's lower torso, hoping to topple him. As Tom fell backwards, he secured his hands around Murphy's throat. He was like a madman, completely out of control. He had one purpose and one purpose only: to get to his family and save them. He held Murphy's neck tight as Murphy gasped for air. He was going to kill him. Weasel was out of options, and a crowd had begun to gather. They were far too conspicuous.

Weasel shouted, "Tom, stop!" and as Tom loosened his grip momentarily on Murphy's neck, Weasel struck him on his head with the butt of his revolver, and his head hit the ground with a thud.

Coughing and rubbing his neck, Murphy helped Weasel launch Tom haphazardly into the back seat. Weasel looked up at the onlookers' agape mouths and glared.

"Be minding your own bloody business, you nosy feckers!"

The people receded from where they had come, some muttering Tom's name in hushed whispers as they went.

Weasel and Murphy piled back into the car and turned away from Palmerstown. Tom's face was frozen in anguish. Weasel struggled to imagine how Tom would cope with the horrifying truth once he woke up to the reality of life without Grace and Sean. They were now indeed kindred spirits, not a soul in the world to call family but each other, on a one-way voyage to America.

* * * *

Major Siddley stared blankly down the stark white corridor of the hospital wing as he waited patiently for Father Ryan to arrive before he could see the boy. The major had assumed that news of the shootings would have reached every corner of Dublin by now, and he had immediately sent troops to scour the city for Thomas Sutton with strict instructions. Considering the recent events, the man is to be arrested and not harmed. He was to be brought directly to him.

Like many of the Irish insurgents before him, Sergeant Armstrong had surmised that Sutton already had a one-way ticket to America. But Siddley couldn't understand how he, a father, could leave his son behind. He must be under the assumption that his son had died. That was the only explanation. He couldn't imagine a father abandoning his son willingly. Like Tom, Siddley had grown up fatherless. His father died in the Burmese War when he was only five, not much younger than Sutton's boy, he suspected. His mother re-married a decade later, but by then, he had almost finished school and had moved on to military training. His stepfather was a gentle, learned man, but it had been too late for them to form a real father-son bond.

He had read Sutton's file in preparation for his impending meeting with the priest and the doctor. He had learned that Tom had been an orphan since the tender age of eight and had practically grown up on the streets. Her parents apparently disowned his wife Grace when she began her courtship with him for obvious reasons. Her parents then migrated to America without further contact, even with their daughter.

He had even asked Armstrong if her parents could be tracked down and contacted. Surely, they would want to take their grandson if Sutton couldn't be found. But Armstrong had noted that her family name was Gallagher, a very common Irish surname. And with no leads on where they eventually settled in America, it would be like retrieving a needle from a haystack. Nonetheless, Armstrong assured the Major that he would try. This left Sutton's boy, Sean was his name, with no living or known relatives. Siddley rubbed his temples in exasperation. What could he do; he felt responsible. Getting Sean Sutton adequate medical attention was insufficient in his mind. He had no idea how traumatized this boy was and what he had seen of his mother's last moments. At least he had been spared the details of his father's death fighting in the war abroad, he thought. This boy had witnessed the inexplicable.

He looked around the waiting room. It was clean and bare; just a few chairs lined up against the wall and a table with the Examiner neatly folded in the middle. He could make out the front page, something about "Death on the Liffey" he sighed heavily and flipped the paper over so he couldn't see the headline anymore. A well-dressed woman wearing a fancy striped, blue hat, a few chairs away from him, cleared her throat, looked up disapprovingly, and turned back to her book.

Siddley had inquired about Sean Sutton's health as soon as he could and was informed that he was weak but had a good chance of recovering from his injuries. The doctor in charge, however, had demanded more information on the boy's background and next of kin. He was only assuaged when Siddley himself told him that he would come to the hospital to explain the situation.

"Did they not have a parish priest?" He had asked Armstrong after reading the file. "These Irish priests seem to know everybody's business; the Irish seem to confide in them more than their own families."

"That, too, is taken care of. He will meet you at the hospital at 6 p.m."

The major appreciated Sergeant Armstrong. He knew that this situation had deeply affected him, and he blamed himself for what had happened.

"I feel responsible for Sean Sutton. If I had arrived thirty minutes earlier, I could have saved his mother and… Lord have mercy on the child… he would not have been robbed of a childhood." He had said with watery eyes when Siddley had left the castle that afternoon.

The major moved uncomfortably in his chair. He was wary of priests. In fact, he wasn't keen on having to talk to this priest at all. But with no family to speak of, this was his only choice. He looked at his watch 18:20. Where was this blasted priest anyway, he thought angrily. No sooner had the thought crossed his mind, but he looked up and saw an intimidating black cassock-robed man clicking down the hallway towards him. He had a carrot-colored beard and a scrutinizing gaze that was fixed in his direction. He walked with purpose. Rising, the major reached out his hand in welcome.

"Good afternoon, Father. Please, won't you have a seat?"

Siddley glanced over at the lady with the hat, who graciously took the cue and exited the waiting room, leaving the men to converse. The priest shook his hand, pulled his chair to the other side of the table, and sat down facing the Major, his expression unmoving. The man's unsettling stare made Siddley nervous, and he wasn't sure why. Was it because he perceived religious men to fear neither life nor death or maybe he was afraid of what he had to say?

"Thank you for coming. Father Ryan, isn't it?"

"It is…thank you, Major." said the priest stoically, with a tight-lipped smile. "I gather I am here for the tragedy which struck the Suttons. Is that correct, Major?"

"Yes, Father," said Siddley, rather surprised by his candidness. "Shouldn't we have met at the morgue instead? I'm not sure how you want me to aid you here, Major. Surely you don't intend for me to present you with Thomas Sutton after the barbarous horror your men inflicted?"

The harsh and cold tone of the priest took major Siddley aback. But they deserved it. He wanted to say that these Black and Tans were never his idea of an army, but that would only muddy the conversation. Instead, he decided to try and appeal to him as a man of the cloth.

"Please, Father, do not make this any more difficult for me. Not all of us are vile, and some of us even have a conscience."

The priest stroked his beard contemplatively and relaxed his countenance. "Apologies, Major. But what do you need from me? I am unaware of Sutton's whereabouts if that's what you're after?"

"No…no, it's not that. I seek your help, Father. That's why I asked you here to the hospital. You see, Sutton's boy, Sean, survived. He is in here recovering."

The priest crossed himself. "Dear God, thank you for letting the child live. That is a blessing indeed."

Siddley paused and lowered his voice. "But he has no one to care for him."

"What about Thomas, his father?" the priest asked earnestly.

"Well, we assume he heard that his family had died. Like you had, Sean included. That's the only thing that makes any sense. And if you don't know where Sutton is, and I don't expect you'd say so anyway, he must be gone. Besides, if he was found Thomas Sutton, you must know that he would be arrested and would likely never see the light of day again." Siddley leaned in with a softer tone. "Is there no kin, or someone close to his mother perhaps who could care for the child? Perhaps a distant relative or friend?"

The priest softened a little. "I am sorry to disappoint you, Major. See, the only relatives the Suttons had were Grace's parents. Grace was a sweet young woman… a very kind soul but always kept to herself, you see. I saw her in mass with her lad Sean often in Lough Tay. You see, I feared that her husband was involved in the violence, and I tried to trace down her parents, for Grace and the boy's sake, in case something ever happened to him. For the past two years, I have contacted loads of churches in America. I assume they must be attending mass somewhere, but I have been unsuccessful so far.

"Then, what about the boy?" asked the major, probing carefully.

"I'll be sayin' 'tis a wicked irony that young Sean Sutton should suffer the same orphan destiny as his father?" he said plainly.

"Look, Father, between you and me, I would sooner see Sutton take his son and get out of Ireland for the good of everyone."

Father Ryan listened attentively, rubbing the cross around his neck.

"But if he has gone, there is nothing I can do. Tell me how I can help the boy. I don't want to see him end up in an orphanage and repeat the cycle."

"It is likely that if Thomas believes his wife and son are dead, he has already left. Wouldn't you? And finding a family of strangers to take the boy, conditions being what they are for most families is unlikely. This land is already brimming with orphans who nobody wants."

The thought of making the boy suffer more due to circumstances that he had no hand in the making angered Siddley.

He rose suddenly and paced back and forth deliberately. "I am sorry, Father, but I cannot digest the thought of Sean being cared for in an orphanage. I am ultimately liable for the actions of my men. Can a man not atone for the sins of others? Cannot something be salvaged here for the sake of this boy?" demanded Siddley with defiance.

Father Ryan's stern gaze softened. "What exactly do you propose, major?" he asked cautiously.

"I can … I can provide for the boy. I can clothe and feed him and give him a roof over his head. How about that?" he stuttered before he could change his mind.

"You, Major? What about his father?" said the priest, who was taken aback at the proposal before him.

"He is not here at this bloody moment to take care of his son, is he? Isn't it better that I care for him until we find Sutton?... Sorry," said Siddley, quickly realizing he had sworn at the priest.

Without skipping a beat, Father Ryan asked, "Tell me, Major, what if you grow too fond of the boy."

"As God is my witness, I will do everything in my power to trace down his father. Even if it takes me twenty years. But until that time, I will care for the boy as my own."

"Even if you are true to word, need I remind you of your profession, Major? 'Tis true that you will not remain in Dublin forever, and you could be transferred at the whim of your government at any time. What then?" posed Father Ryan seriously.

"That is likely, Father. But if Sutton has indeed escaped to another land and I am transferred to another post, I will no longer be bound to arrest him. And regardless of where I go, I will continue to search for his father, man to man, and not for retribution. And when that day comes, I will return Sean to the care of his biological father. I am a man of my word, Father."

"Major, you do know that you don't need my permission to adopt the boy." the priest said honestly.

"But consider the circumstances...I need your blessing before I take him from his country, from his people. Think about my offer, Father. It is the best for the boy." and with that, they both rose.

Siddley shook the priest's hand and gestured to the door. "Let's go and see the boy, shall we, Father?"

"Yes, let us see the boy."

Father Ryan was convinced that the Major felt for the boy. Aside from the remorse he clearly felt over Grace's death and Sean's situation, maybe the major had some wound in his past that was also pulling at his heart. But was it the right decision to let Sean Sutton live in the care of a British Major when his father had fought so relentlessly against their occupation? And could the Major really put aside the quest to bring Thomas to justice for this boy's sake? But then again, hadn't the bible taught him that men could change and love could conquer all? Hadn't the injured traveler been saved by the Samaritan, his enemy? Maybe something good could come from this tragedy somehow.

Neither he nor Siddley spoke as they walked through the corridors of the hospital to where Sean was convalescing. Both were lost in deep thoughts of their own. Major Siddley knew that he was about to meet a barrage of questions from the doctor, and he had hoped to be on better footing with the priest at this point. When they neared the casualty ward, the doctor attending to Sean approached the Major. He was a tall, thin, balding man with a no-nonsense demeanor. He held a clipboard close to his white starch uniform, and his unruly black eyebrows shifted upwards as he saw the Major and the priest approaching. He wasted no time getting to his point and did not offer his hand.

"Major Siddley, I am glad to have you here in person finally. Your office has not been very forthcoming. The only information I was able to gather from your sergeant was that the boy's father had been a soldier and that his name was Sean. No details on his mother. I need more information."

The Major didn't take the bait but gestured to the priest beside him instead. "Doctor, this is Father Ryan. The circumstances of the boy's situation are unfortunately classified at the moment. The Father here can corroborate that the boy has no known family, and given that he is now likely an orphan, Father Ryan will be deemed his next of kin until a suitable situation can be established."

Siddley hoped that the priest would play along, and he did by nodding affirmatively to the man.

Recognizing that he was not going to get any more information, the doctor nodded at the priest and then referred to his clipboard.

Without giving either of them any eye contact, he proceeded. "Very well then…please follow me. I will tell you that the boy believes his father is a hero."

As they entered the room, the sight of the little boy nestled in a big bed clenched Siddley's heart in a way he hadn't expected. He looked so small and helpless. Soon, he would wake to find himself all alone in this world. He coughed to clear the lump in his throat and looked pleadingly at the priest. Father Ryan returned his gaze and contemplated his choices. The Major had assured him that Sean would be kept safe, and he was sure he could check in on the child's welfare from time to time. He knew that Sean's life would certainly be bleak if he was forced into an orphanage, especially after the trauma he had endured. He feared for the boy's future. What choice did he have but to offer this up to God?

As they both stood at the bottom of Sean's bed, the priest looked at the major and uttered two words. "I agree."

CHAPTER 8

A Change of Course

ven the strongest spirit can be crushed. He opened his eyes a crack, hoping he was dead and that he had passed on to some other place. His head was heavy, and it felt bruised on the inside. The room was swaying ever so slightly. He closed his eyes again. Maybe the world would go away and leave him be. Inside, he ached with grief he could not smother. He had been so close, and God had taken from him everything he had ever loved. He squeezed his eyes tighter. Maybe he could just fade away into nothingness and disappear. Everything he had done had been meaningless- he had lost the love of his life. He was living a nightmare worse than any he could have conjured.

Several minutes passed, and then, against his better judgement, he unsealed his eyelids and let his surroundings materialize through the blur. To his right was a wooden table with a basin and towel. He appeared to be lying on the wooden bunk bed, but the opposite wall was only six feet away. His pillow was wet with sweat. He was hot and reeked of liquor. Above him, another body moved, making the bed over his head creak. Hearing his own voice for the first time in what seemed like days, he slurred in a grave tone that he didn't recognize.

"Where in the name of the devil are we, Weasel? And why is it so bloody dark and hot in here?"

Weasel's disheveled mop emerged from the top bunk above him. "At Sea." He stated in a matter-of-fact tone and disappeared as fast as he had appeared.

"I had gathered that from the way we were swaying," said Tom with a frustrated grunt as his temples ached unbearably. "But what the bloody hell are we doing on a ship? I told you I would not go to America, Weasel."

The voice from the beyond replied dismissively. "We are not going to America, Tom. You can relax."

Weasel's reply satisfied Tom momentarily, and he reclined back on his moist pillow, which smelled like stale whisky and sweat, and adjusted it angrily. Now lying on his back with his hands behind his head, he stared at the bottom of Weasel's bunk. His faculties were returning to him, and his tone was quieter this time.

"How many days have we been at sea?"

"Hard to tell. It's been a while since we left Southampton," came the voice from above.

"Southampton?" Tom's eyes widened in alarm. He searched his memory but had no recollection of having been there.

"Yes, Tom. Southampton," said Weasel methodically like he was talking to a small child

"England?"

"No, Scotland... Of course, England, you eejit!" Weasel answered agitatedly, wondering if he was ever going to see the Tom Sutton he had once known again or if he was destined to travel with a mere shell of the man who sustained himself on a daily quotient of whiskey to forget he was alive.

Tom was oblivious to the irritation in Weasel's voice and, sitting up now, ploughed forward with his questions, trying to make some sense of it all. His head pounded.

"How long since we left Southampton?"

"You don't even remember that much? Jaysus… seven days, my friend."

"Seven days? Eh, where the hell are we going?"

Seeing that Tom was asking coherent and sustained questions, Weasel turned to lie on his side and propped himself on his elbow, answering hopefully.

"To Africa. Do you know this is the first time you have spoken words that have made any sense since we left Dublin?"

"Africa?" mumbled Tom. His head pounded, and he was having a hard time focusing.

Weasel was exasperated. His face became hot, and he swung his legs over the edge and bounded to the floor, unleashing all the pent-up frustration he had bottled for the last week trying to manage Tom Sutton.

"Yes! Bloody Africa? Look at you, for God's sake. You're the very depiction of the word shame! You've been a bloody drunkard ever since we left Palmerstown. Don't you remember? Murphy and I did only what friends are supposed to do, but you fought us like we were the bloody Black and Tans!"

Tom looked at his friend like a frightened child, blinking his eyes, trying to focus on the shiner on Weasel's left eye.

"So, you want to bloody well know why we're heading to Africa? Because you put up a fit that America would not be the same without Grace and Sean, which earned me this." Weasel rubbed his black eye.

"You said you'd go anywhere, be it Australia, China or Africa… so here we are on the Durham Castle, heading to the Cape."

Tom flopped back on the pillow and screwed his eyes shut to stop the tears which flowed freely now as he attempted to devolve back into the depths from which he had come. Weasel sighed deeply, realizing he had touched a nerve by mentioning their names.

Sitting down on the edge of Tom's bed, he patted his shoulder gently. "Well, we don't speak Chinese, so we're going to Africa." Weasel's attempt at humor was of no use. Tom had already retreated to his dark place and had begun to mumble again.

"They killed them for my sins. And you know something, I will kill you all, Weasel, for taking me from them when they needed me," he cried.

Weasel had hoped he'd seen the last of these episodes. When he got like this, Weasel didn't know how to bring him back from this darkness. He somberly rose and whispered, "You will understand why I had to, Tom, one day."

"Where's my bottle?" demanded Sutton, suddenly grabbing his wrist without opening his eyes.

"Where is my fecking whisky? I want it now, goddamn you." Tom let go of Weasel and started slipping back into a semi-conscious state. Weasel couldn't stand to see this man he had so admired decline like this. He couldn't even come to grips with the death of his wife and son without wallowing in the bottle. He remembered how Tom had rescued him from losing his mind when Shamus died. He understood the anguish. But it had been going on like this for two weeks, and he was losing hope of ever getting the man back.

Weasel grabbed Tom forcefully by the shoulders. "Look at me! I said, look at me. You are a disgrace, Tom Sutton. You brought me back from the torment of losing my brother. I understand the pain...I do. But just look at yourself! Grace and Sean would be ashamed of the drunkard you have become. You sully their memory. You have lost all self-respect. It's been more than a week, and you need to snap out of this boyo. Where is the Thomas Sutton we all admired?" cried Weasel hopelessly.

Tears welled up in Tom's eyes, and his lips quivered. Somewhere in the recesses of his mind, he saw Weasel sobbing at the edge of the bed in Maggie's place. If Weasel didn't care for him, he wouldn't be here right now. That much was clear. He suddenly felt sober, soberer at least than he had in days.

"I'm sorry. Let's get off at the next port and go back to Dublin. I promise I will sober up, and then we can avenge all their deaths. You're the closest thing to the family that I have left. Don't give up on me."

He sobbed loudly, shut his eyes, and reached out his hand. "Now, hand me the Jameson, mate."

Weasel's optimism was instantly shattered. Shaking his head disapproving, he surrendered and handed him another bottle of whiskey. He knew if he were to deny Tom his drink, the man would put up a fight, and he didn't have the stomach for it. He watched despondently as Tom greedily gulped down the liquid as it trickled down his chin.

"Sure, drown your sorrows and hurt the ones you are with, Tom," mumbled Weasel to himself, wondering if the courageous man he had once known would ever surface again. Grabbing a booklet from his bag, he crept back up to his bunk, talking to himself. "I suppose I will just keep meself company and bury my nose in this book to figure what port we are headed to next in South Africa."

If it's true that time heals all wounds, then the deeper the wound, the longer the time. Countless men and women had laid down their lives for Ireland in hopes of freeing her from foreign rule. The wounds were deep for so many. A couple of months after they arrived in Cape Town, Weasel and Tom received news from Murphy of a police raid at a Gaelic football match between Dublin and Tipperary, where fourteen spectators were killed. Tom and Weasel surmised it had probably been in retaliation for attacks by the IRA, although Murphy never mentioned that.

Over the next two years, Ireland had a domino of incidents. First came Bloody Sunday in the Fall of 1920, which was followed by Marshall Law two weeks later in four counties. De Valera sent Michael Collins to England in July to negotiate the 1921 Anglo-Irish Treaty to establish a free state. The treaty required an Oath of Allegiance to the British Crown, which De Valera couldn't justify. However, Collins persuaded most of the revolutionary parliament to ratify the treaty. A month later, he was assassinated by Anti-Treaty forces, and the Irish Civil War was re-ignited. For the year that followed, countrymen killed fellow countrymen, claiming more lives than the fight for independence that had preceded it. Seeing the conflict that they had been instrumental in starting play out over these last two years made Tom wonder if he could have stomached it all or if he would have even survived it. They had been an integral part of that fight for self-rule. But reading it now in black and white print, on a dock thousands of miles away on another continent, seemed surreal.

Tom was sure that if freedom ever came, those who survived would come out to bid adieu to the retreating British soldiers as their ships departed from Dublin's North Wall. Oh, how he wished he could be there to see it for himself. But his wounds reminded him that a bitter resentment would live on in the hearts of generations to come for the pain this freedom had wrought. This pain of hid, pain two years later, remained insufferable.

* * * *

It had been almost four and half years since Major Siddley had been stationed at Dublin Castle, fresh from Picardy and the Battle of Amiens. He honestly hadn't expected his tour to be longer than a year, but here he was, some four years later, packing up his flat to return home.

He had been true to his word, and despite the anguish and bloodshed in the fight for Irish Independence, he had spent the last two years searching for Thomas Sutton. Despite the search, he had received no tips as to his whereabouts. He had simply vanished into thin air. If he had escaped, America had seemed like the most logical destination, given the family connection, but his efforts to find him had come up moot. The man had either simply chosen to save himself and leave his past behind him or, what Siddley deemed more likely, was painfully unaware of a living son.

For two and half years, Siddley had raised Sean as his own, just as he had promised Father Ryan. After a couple of months, the priest checked in on him far less frequently now, satisfied by the arrangement that he believed was in the boy's best interest.

It was with a heavy heart that the major had watched the boy's lip tremble that first day when he revealed that his mother had died and his father could not be found. Siddley had gone back to Tom's house in Palmerstown and retrieved his mother's trunk so Sean might find some comfort in some tangible things from his childhood. He continually appeased the boy by promising Sean that he would continue to search for his father, although he believed in his heart that the effort was likely futile.

Tragically, Sean recalled the home invasion vividly and wet the bed for the first six months during fitful nightmares. As months turned into years, the nightmares subsided, and the boy spoke less of his father. However, he became withdrawn and would spend hours alone in his room, rifling through his mother's things again and again.

Despite his baggage, Sean was quite mature for his age, and from the beginning, he understood that this man, the major, who had taken him in had the best intentions. He was cognizant that life at an orphanage would be far worse, and he tried to show his appreciation with obedience. But he was keenly aware that he was an Irish boy living with a British Military "father" who couldn't shield him from the violence he'd seen with his own eyes and heard almost every day on the radio since. He was conflicted in every way, and the major knew it.

Because Sean struggled to focus on school, the major hired a tutor. He was a young University student who liked to hear the sound of his own voice too much, Sean thought. For three hours each day, he endured lessons in arithmetic, geography, history, and science, and that kept his mind off things mostly. In the afternoons, the housekeeper Mrs. Shields, took care of him. She was a twitchy middle-aged woman with rosy cheeks who flustered easily. But she was kind to him and listened to his stories without ever scolding him. She even let him help her in the kitchen, which made him feel nostalgic, and he was grateful for that.

But the nights were always painful. Each night, like a ritual, he lay in his bed and tried to see his mother's eyes, her smiling green eyes like his own, Father Ryan had said. He could almost feel her hand tousling his hair like she used to. Then he searched for his father, and he would always find him running from the scene to save himself, leaving him and his mother behind with all the blood and mess and pain. He would sometimes muffle his screams into his pillow. He hated him.

Siddley not only felt it was his penance to protect and care for this boy, but he had also grown to love him like a son and affectionately addressed him as John, perhaps subconsciously hoping he could create a new future for him. When it had come time for Major Siddley to return home to England. The Sutton's tragedy had become just another casualty of war-torn Palmerstown, and it was clear that if Sean stayed, he would have no future here, especially as an orphan. Father Ryan had warmed to Siddley over the past two and half years and, a few months after Grace's tragic death had given him his blessing to legally adopt John Sutton Siddley.

Sean liked the name John. It felt like a new beginning, and he, too, wanted a fresh start. In some ways, he felt like moving to England was a defiance of everything his father stood for, and that made him feel good. Before they left, Father Ryan gave Sean a photograph of him with his mother and father taken outside the church.

"Don't forget who you are, Sean. You were loved. You are still loved." he said with a pat on the head.

In the photo, his father, Tom Sutton, had one arm around his mother and his other hand on his shoulder. It was the day of his Holy Communion and the last time they had been together as a family in public. He remembered now that Father Ryan had performed the sacrament in the rectory long after mass, for him alone, so his father could be there. It had been Grace's request.

Sometimes, Sean would run his fingers over the wrinkles in the paper, wondering if they had ever been happy together. In his dreams, he still clung to the happy memories of the cottage in Lough Tay. Even images of a father who once loved him by the lake invaded his mind from time to time before he shook them loose. He had so many questions for his father and so much anger. But right now, he has accepted the major as his guardian. He had been good to him, so he would go to England with him, maybe never to return to the land of his birth and past. And so, with one final breath of Irish air at Dublin's North Wall, John took the major's hand and boarded the ferry for Holyhead.

CHAPTER 9

Heidi Van Wyk

Words are not bound to time and place. The printed word travels effortlessly across human boundaries that divide lands, people, and generations. Such were the words that found their way to Tom's ears as Weasel stumbled ecstatically over the headlines of *The Cape Times* early one December morning in 1922. Fitting news from a paper that had been started by one of their countrymen, a man named Frederick St. Leger from Limerick. Weasel sprang from his seat with enthusiasm, nearly knocking over his tea, giving life to the words on the page. Ireland had been liberated from the British Empire!

The civil war had been won by the pro-treaty Free State forces. All three provinces of Leinster, Munster, and Connaught, and County Donegal in the north west of Ulster, for a total of 26 counties, became known as the Free State. The minority who was in favor of British rule entitled the remaining six counties of Ulster to be under the rule of the British Empire. It was over. All their collective efforts had been worth it, after all. But had they? Tom wondered. What had he gained for all the sacrifice?

This news of liberation from across the ocean should have evinced feelings of celebration, but without his family, the news was empty and disconnected for Tom. Over these many months, when memories of the past and thoughts of what-ifs crowded his mind, he would simply drown them out with a gulp of whisky.

Alcohol had taken a toll on his wretched body, and he had become a sad replica of his former self. He was wafer thin, and shallow cheeks and a vacant look now replaced his once strong jaw and handsome face. He cared not for his appearance and barely bothered to bathe or groom himself anymore. If it weren't for Weasel, he would have simply wasted away in some dank corner, invisible to the world around him- the way he wanted to be.

He only ate at Weasel's nagging behest and out of fear of the landlady, Mrs. Baldwin, who scowled visibly if her meals were not devoured with appropriate appreciation. Weasel kept Tom's drinking as inconspicuous at the boarding house as possible and was forever reminding him that his job, too, was on the line if they suspected Tom was drunk. It was bad enough that he had earned a reputation as the resident drunkard from his fellow dock workers, both African and Dutch, who glanced at him sideways as he left with his nightly bottle of spirit. Tom had no retort for the jeering, but Weasel only wished they could have seen him in his prime. Tom did still care about one thing-Weasel. He agreed to eat and follow the prescribed rules for him alone. He didn't want to disappoint Weasel. He needed him, and Weasel was all he had.

It had been two years, one month, and 21 days since their deaths. For the past two years, he had worked side by side with Weasel at a dock in Cape Town, lifting, carrying, and piling cargo. Both had lost their families and had no specific destination in mind when they started this journey, so this place seemed as good as any.

The weather was lovely, with a temperature of 72 degrees this Sunday morning, and there was not a cloud in the eggshell blue sky. Clean, white light streamed through the window, and Tom closed his eyes for a moment and let the sunshine wash over him. This was the only thing that made Tom feel alive. He loved the morning sun, especially outside on the dock. It always felt invigorating and renewing. But inevitably, as the day drew on, these feelings devolved into sweat and nights of drunken sleep. Weasel peered at him across the table, over *The Cape Times* in the dining room of their boarding house. It was in these sober moments that Weasel saw glimpses of his best friend.

Tom didn't linger long on the news of Ireland's liberation but toasted the emancipation with a mug of tea and a bite of toast before launching into another familiar harangue about how grateful he was to have the option of Irish whiskey and the virtues of the spirit from the motherland. And like that, Tom was gone again.

As Tom ranted on familiarly, Weasel catalogued the last two years. He had never imagined Tom's grief would have lasted so long in this way. He had thought, over time, these new surroundings would have eased his suffering, but the anonymity only seemed to facilitate his withdrawal from society. With each passing day, he seemed farther from saving, and Weasel's impotent attempts to get him clean only ended in fights. Weasel naturally blamed himself for Tom's drinking habit. Sometimes, he wanted to do nothing more than escape the sight of the broken man, but Tom's daily declaration to Weasel was his only family and that he loved him like a brother always stopped him from going.

In the darkest hours, Weasel would even close his eyes and try to reach Grace in prayer, not that he had ever been much of a religious sort, and he would hear her words reflected on him.

"I know no words can console or compensate you for the loss of family, especially your brother. I hope you know that we are your family now, always and forever." And so, for her, he stayed.

Just like this morning, Weasel had learned to drown out Tom's melancholia as he relived Grace and Sean's deaths repeatedly. He had given up trying to steer the conversation to the present or hearken to happier times. Even this recent news of the liberation had had little effect on his spirit. The atmosphere around Tom was suffocating. Weasel wished he could make him see that their families would have wanted them to live, to rebuild, to start over. But there was no convincing Tom of this.

As he read the newspaper, Weasel simply repeated the familiar mantra, "In due time, Sutton… in due time, you'll recover." Tom stared out the window, mumbling. It couldn't possibly go on like this indefinitely, could it? Weasel wondered.

Weasel took Tom directly to his room after supper and put him to bed, bottle and all. He had learned his lesson the first few months in this strange place, scouring the seedy dockside bars and places of ill repute looking for his friend into the early morning.

He had suffered nightmares of finding Tom's body face down in a gutter along the dock after a night of debauchery he barely remembered. In his intemperate state, he was unknowingly damaging the once-stainless reputation of a courageous leader and faithful and devoted husband in favor of being a common dipsomaniac.

Some mornings, when he was mostly sober, Tom would stare out over the ocean at the dock and spin Weasel a tale of turning over a new leaf. He would promise to stop his consumption of whiskey, and Weasel would cling to hope time and again, only to be rejected at dusk, when Tom purchased another bottle and settled into another night, making love to his whiskey and drowning out any hope for change.

Despite this monumental news from the motherland, their typical Sunday morning routine remained the same. A period of sobriety during breakfast was followed by a walk-through of town in the fresh air. Like any other Sunday, the blue sky and sunshine had born a new set of promises and declarations that Weasel knew Tom would not keep by sunset. Before dinnertime, Weasel found himself carefully escorting his drunken friend up the wooden staircase of their boarding home. Meticulously attempting not to draw too much attention from privy eyes.

"Can you manage to get yourself undressed? I'll go and fetch you some dinner," whispered Weasel at his door.

"It's fine…you…can go," Sutton slurred in response. "I don't think so."

"I am fine, Weasel. I feel refreshed."

Weasel smiled sadly and took a step back as he watched his friend stumble through the doorway into his room. Tom could be cheerful when he was drunk, and it was at those moments of levity that Weasel grasped for the old Tom before he descended into despair. As Tom retreated to the safety of his wrecked room, the door closed, and Weasel turned solemnly downstairs. Placing the whiskey next to the bed, Tom pulled off his clothes, stumbling over his left trouser leg as he flung it to the side into a pile of other clothes. Wasting not another moment, he collapsed on the single bed before him, and, pulling the sheets above his head, he closed his bloodshot eyes. His erratic heartbeat calmed into a steady rhythm as his mind started drifting into slumber. As he clung to the last moments of consciousness, he wondered if his life was even worth saving or if he was destined to live in this repetitive hell.

Every soul has the capacity for salvation. Redemption isn't a miracle, but a choice and grace are free to anyone with the courage to take it. Tom was given such a choice a mere hour or so into his slumber. Something forced him awake. He unsealed his weary eyes to reveal a little girl standing in the doorway, lit only by the dim light that filtered in from the hallway outside. He struggled to focus. Was he dreaming? Was this an angel visitor? As his eyes began to focus, he saw that she was carrying a bowl larger than her hands.

She said nothing but only stared at him with inquisitive blue eyes. Who was this intruder who had come without a simple knock or greeting? He was suddenly aware of his naked chest and sat up, pulling the sheet tight around himself. The floor between him and the child was a squalid mess of strewn whiskey bottles, piles of dirty clothes, and overflowing ashtrays. He looked annoyingly at her. He was embarrassed. She said nothing.

Tom glanced at the clock on the wall and saw that it was still evening. He had barely slept an hour or two. With each passing second, he felt more and more uncomfortable and alert as the little girl just stood in the doorway. He straightened up in bed and ran his hands through his hair in an attempt to appear more presentable.

The little girl cleared her throat before speaking sweetly in a sing-song Afrikaans accent. "Mr. Sutton, Mrs. Baldwin sent me up with some soup for you."

Tom tilted his head in response and squinted his eyes in confusion. He also cleared his throat and spoke politely in hopes of masking how shameful he felt. He noted that these feelings of shame were new.

"Who are you, child?"

"My name is Heidi, Mr. Sutton." "Pardon me, Heidi, who?"

The girl spoke with a confident smile, "Heidi Van Wyk."

Tom instructed the girl to take a few steps forward so that he could see her better, to which the girl obliged.

"Well, it's very nice to make your acquaintance, Heidi Van Wyk," said Tom with a small bow from his bed.

The girl chuckled, and Tom smiled back. He hadn't felt this disarmed since he had last seen Sean. She was dressed plainly in a knee-length cotton brown dress and was barefoot, although she didn't seem to mind. Her pretty round face was kissed with the sun, and freckles dotted her nose. Her eyes were round and deep blue and her wavy yellow hair cascaded onto her shoulders. He guessed that she was about seven, the same age Sean was when he had last seen him.

"Heidi Van Wyk, you say. Well, what can I do for you this evening, Heidi?"

Heidi approached the bed, navigating her way through the mess to place the bowl on his bedside table while Tom embarrassedly swept scraps of old newspapers, a dirty sock, and some careless cigarette butts off the table to accommodate.

Placing the bowl, Heidi continued without stopping, "Mrs. Baldwin instructed me to bring you this bowl of soup. She said you would not be coming to the dining room tonight and that you better stay locked up here. She said her dining room is better off without you, and you're no good of a person."

Watching the little girl deliver the elderly's complaint so plainly and brutally made Tom erupt in laughter, catching them both off-guard. She laughed, too, and then took a seat on the foot of the bed. Tom hadn't heard himself laugh in a lifetime. It felt good. He felt alive.

Once their hilarity subsided, Heidi gestured to the bowl sternly, wagging her finger and speaking in giggles.

"Will you indeed finish your soup, Mr. Sutton?"

"Yes, I will, Heidi," Tom said genuinely with a smile. Her next question caught him off-guard.

"Would you care for some whiskey, Mr. Sutton?" "Good Lord, why would you ask that lass?" "Because I pour my father his whiskey."

"Why?"

"He drinks a lot sometimes. He is sick."

Tom uttered an apology to the girl, who was quick to wave it away before excusing herself.

"Well, I best not take up your time, Mr. Sutton. Do you want that whiskey?"

"No, Heidi. No, thank you …at least not tonight."

"Mr. Sutton, it is deemed improper for a young lady to visit a man unaccompanied in his bedroom. You, however, are most welcome to come to visit me, Mr. Sutton. My father and I are in room fifteen."

Tom was taken aback by her boldness but touched by her extension of friendship. "Well, thank you for the kind invitation, Heidi. When, shall I come to visit you?"

"Any time is fine, Mr. Sutton," said Heidi cheerfully, and with that, she clapped her hands together, rose, and walked to the door, which remained ajar.

Before exiting the room, she turned to Tom and sincerely offered him those words of redemption. "Mr. Sutton, I don't believe you're no good of a person…I just thought you should know."

Her words caught him off-guard. He didn't realize how much her validation could mean against the common perception that he was indeed dishonorable. He smiled in return and muttered incoherent words in Afrikaans under her breath. Her little frame disappeared as she shut the door behind her. Tom sat in his bed for a moment, dumbfounded and surprisingly sober. Something about Heidi had made him care again. Something about her made him want to be sober.

As the effects of intoxication continued to wear off, his mind came alive. Images of his life in the cottage flashed before him. This time, the memories were happy ones. The cottage, the lake, the fields, Sean's laughter, and Grace's red hair entangled in his fingers overwhelmed his sober mind. Tears sprung freely, but these weren't tears of death and despair. They were tears of joy and thankfulness. He understood why he had wanted Heidi to stay. She reminded him so much of his Sean. He knew his son was dead, but Heidi's visit had conjured happy memories, memories he had intentionally suffocated out of self-hate.

A waterfall of tears soaked his cheeks and bare chest while a mix of emotions stirred within him. Remorse, guilt, grief, fury, and, most importantly, regret raged in his heart. He did something he had not done for years. He prayed.

"I am so sorry, Grace and Sean, for not being there to protect you. I am sorry you were punished for my actions. I would give anything to turn back time, my darling wife, and give you the life you deserved. I am sorry I disappointed you, Grace, but I want you to know that I will always love you from the depths of my soul. You will forever be my compass and guide. And Sean, I am not the brave soldier that you thought I was. But I promise that I will try to be a good man. You shall forever be my anchor son."

He wiped his eyes with the bed sheet and looked around the room at the disorder he had brought into his life. Then he thought of Weasel. Weasel had never left his side, but he had constantly shut him out and made promises he never kept. His heart tugged at the thought of hurting Weasel one more time.

This little stranger's simple words of kindness had worked like a spell to unchain his heart. Then he thought of her, bound to an ailing father, who was also apparently a drunkard. Drunkard: he had always despised that word. What would Sean think of a drunkard for a father? He felt ashamed.

He reached for the bottle on his bedside table. He could only see Heidi and Sean as he raised it to his lips. With a guttural scream, he launched the bottle across the room, where it landed with a clang.

He breathed deeply and resolutely and reached for the bowl of soup. He surveyed his room and promised himself he would do a deep cleaning in the morning. He took note of his own odor and, with a chuckle, promised himself a bath. He mused about the words Heidi had muttered as she left the room. I must ask Weasel what that means, he wondered; Weasel's Afrikaans were pretty decent. He decided the soup was pretty average, but the redemption taste was unequalled.

CHAPTER 10

The Dutchman

Mrs. Baldwin's eyes nearly bulged from their sockets when a clean-shaven, decently groomed Thomas Sutton descended the boarding house staircase the following morning.

"I hope you found the soup last night to your satisfaction, Mr. Sutton?" she managed to expel through pursed lips, maintaining the authoritative composure that usually commanded her hen-pecked husband.

Tom simply smiled and tipped his hat. "'T'was awe-inspiring, Madam," he said charmingly with a wink that instantly disarmed her, and she bustled off to the kitchen flustered.

Weasel took note of the drastic change in Tom's demeanor and appearance and was instantly suspicious. As soon as they were outside the boarding house, he began to question him. Jogging to keep up with Tom's pace.

"What's with that ageing maiden?"

"Mrs. Baldwin? Nothing, she wants my money." Tom said with a smile and started to whistle cheerfully as he continued to walk purposefully towards the dock.

"Your money? Pardon me, but I recall you have generously donated all of yours to those great Irish whiskey makers, John Power & Sons, and of course Jamison"

"Well, then I'll have to work harder today. I'm meeting some-one special tonight." Tom smiled and winked at Weasel.

"As the word "special" escaped Tom's lips, Weasel's eyes wid-ened in bewilderment. He stopped momentarily and then hurried to catch up with his friend. He was intrigued that such a transfor-mation could have occurred overnight, and who was this mysteri-ous woman who could have brought his friend back from the dead? Ecstatic at the prospect but nonetheless decidedly skeptical, Weasel questioned if he was, in truth, catering to a lady that evening. Tom smiled mischievously.

"What a lady! No, I'm going to meet a leprechaun." "Sutton… I am your friend!" Weasel exclaimed.

For two years, Weasel had witnessed almost every waking min-ute of Tom's life. The fact that he had been kept out of this secret was killing him, and Tom was relishing in it.

"My friend?" Tom teased. "Didn't realize that." "You know that I am, Tom."

"Then give me two pounds. I want to present her with some-thing of brilliance, unlike anything she has ever seen."

Weasel felt slightly betrayed. Weasel's pace slowed, and he looked deflated. Upon reaching the dock, Tom recognized that his joke was causing more injury than he had meant it to, and he stopped to let Weasel catch up.

"She is just a little girl…only seven or eight, Weasel," Tom said, laughing as he slapped him playfully on the shoulder.

"Who? That little lass that brought you dinner last night?" said Weasel, piecing it together.

"Yes, that's right, a little girl Weasel…not a lady." Tom smiled and looked Weasel in the eyes now, his tone changing. "Now you know that Grace was the one and only girl in my life. But last night, I realized that all this time, I had buried myself with her and Sean's memory. I had forgotten how to laugh… until that little girl taught me how to again. I've felt so guilty all this time that I had forgotten how to feel. But that's a dishonor to their memories. I can't bring them back, but I can choose to live. I can choose to do good." Tom's eyes were watery, but he was smiling, and they were bright and sober.

Weasel had waited so patiently for this rebirth, this turn of the tide for Tom. For two long years, he had waited and had almost given up on his friend umpteen times, only to remind himself that he was his only family now, and you don't abandon your family. But this was different. He could see that Tom's newfound clarity was real and sober. This was not like the other times when Tom would rally and make empty promises about the future, only to dissolve in a bottle of whisky by suppertime.

For the first time, he acknowledged the past and honored it for what it was - the past. Weasel smiled broadly and threw his arms around Tom in a bear hug, which Tom heartily returned. Weasel knew the bottle would be hard to kick, but at least he had real tangible hope that Tom could make his way back to the world of the living.

The men continued to chat as they boarded the recently docked cargo ship and began unloading crates and boxes. Tom recounted his conversation with Heidi the previous night. He searched Weasel for the meaning of the Afrikaans words Heidi had muttered objectively as she had left his room the night before. *"Hierdie plek lyk so's 'n hond se stert!"* *

Weasel translated, "This place looks like a dog's tail," and they both laughed until their sides hurt. Only children could get away with being so brutally honest.

"Perhaps I should do something about it." snorted Tom, trying to suppress his laughter."

"You should, Thomas. Your room is a pigsty, a right filthy one at that."

"Well, thank you!" laughed Tom sarcastically. "And I'm sure I didn't smell too pretty either."

"I'd personally like to thank the lass for shaming you into a bath. It's about time. I am happy to have you back. Tom and I are grateful to this little girl, whoever she is, for being able to do what I couldn't."

An easy banter between the men continued throughout the day. As they worked, they joked and laughed like old times. Weasel continued to look for signs of a backslide but saw none and remained cautiously optimistic that this was indeed a new chapter.

He had also been thinking of the future. He thought he would broach the topic on the way home.

"So, what about going back to our Motherland then, Thomas?" said Weasel carefully as they left the dock.

Tom felt queasy. This had been a big day for him, and he sensed that Weasel wanted to jump at the chance to seize the moment. He did, however, wish that neither of them should ever feel bound by the other. If Weasel wanted to go back to Ireland, Tom would not stop him. However, he wasn't sure if he really did or just thought it best for Tom's sake. Surviving hadn't been easy in Cape Town, and their futures here held little opportunity.

"Byrne, look, these feelings are all new to me, and I'm still trying to figure it all out. You know I will always love Ireland, but I'm afraid I have nothing there anymore, or rather no one to go back to now. My home is buried with Grace and Sean. I know the road ahead won't be easy, but I can start a new life here. So, I've decided to stay here.

Maybe I'll head to the north for an adventure or two. Maybe I'll witness some of the majestic sights this vast continent offers. Either way, I plan to take each day as it comes and try to find some peace in this world until I'm finally reunited with my wife and son.

Do you know that little girl Heidi cares for a sick, drunk father in that godforsaken boarding house? But she still smiles and laughs and lives each day like it's blessed. I, too, can bury my miseries and take on each new day with resolve and make the best out of this life of mine. But I can't do it there. It's too painful. So, I'm afraid I won't be going back, my friend…my brother." Tom said sadly.

Weasel looked him over and gave him a disapproving look.

"What do you mean, will I? Are you old enough to be without my supervision and wisdom? I'll let you know that I cared for you all these months. You cannot get rid of me this easily as my middle age approaches. I'm afraid we are two peas in a pod now, my friend… my brother."

Tom's face erupted in a grin, and he threw his hand over Weasel's shoulder. The two walked in matching steps home to the boarding house.

Tom kept Weasel to his word on the two pounds, and on the way home, they stopped by a shop on Adderley Street that imported fine china and figurines. He bought Heidi a little music box with an angel perched upon it. The cherub's golden locks and blue eyes reminded him of her, and he thought the figure fitting for the occasion.

Her blue eyes lit up that night when Tom visited her and her father in room fifteen. As she laid eyes on the little angel, she squealed in delight.

"Thank you, Mister Sutton, oh thank you." she said, throwing her little arms around his neck."

Heidi's father, Charles A. Van Wyk, looked on from his bed with a smile. Tom could tell he had once been a substantial man. Heidi had inherited his piercing eyes and golden hair, although unlike hers, his hair was thinning and had lost its luster. His illness, conflated by his alcohol consumption, had taken a toll on his once robust frame, and his skin was ashen and his face gaunt.

He was a gentleman, and he loved Heidi furiously, which was evident in the way he engaged her interminable chatter and gathered her to him with kisses and embraces every chance he had. His honesty, straightforwardness, and unconditional love had imbued the little girl with a strength beyond her years, for it was clear that Van Wyk would only be a guest for a few more months in this world.

Tom was always impressed by the way Charles made an effort. He was always washed, dressed, and groomed. His whiskey habit, he discovered, was a means to navigate the pain he endured as a tumor in his brain ravaged his mind and body. Tom could sense his agony, but the man always put on a brave face for his daughter. This made Tom feel ashamed for how he had allowed himself to decline over the past two years and for how he had felt sorry for himself.

Tom came to enjoy the company of both father and daughter. Every night, he would stop up to room fifteen for a visit before supper.

Sometimes, Heidi would read to them both, narrating and acting out all the parts to grand applause. Sometimes, when Tom sensed that Van Wyk was feeling more poorly than usual, he and Heidi would play checkers or work on a puzzle together, laughing and chattering as her father looked on. Sometimes, even Weasel would join in, and the four would share stories and delight in Heidi's wild imaginings.

Tom naturally grew fond of Heidi. Her infusion of light and life kept him off the drink. It was silly, but he wanted her to be proud of him. Van Wyk came to understand the scars Tom shielded and keenly observed how Heidi had somehow filled some void within him. As the man slowly deteriorated, Tom would often visit him after Heidi was asleep. He found his late-night chats with the man rather therapeutic. He was older than Tom but at least a decade, having married later in life. He seemed almost like a father figure to Tom.

Charles was always anxious to learn more about his past and contemplate his future, which helped Tom sort out his feelings. Tom had never found it easy to share his deepest thoughts before with anyone but Grace, but maybe it was Van Wyk's vulnerability that coaxed it out of him. Half the time, the man was in a half-sleep, and Tom wasn't sure if he even heard him, which admittedly made it easier.

Tom sensed that they shared a similar pain, and their conversations soon became effortless. Tom told him of his difficult orphan childhood and his fight for a free Ireland. He didn't divulge his reasons for leaving, only that his wife and son had died, and the Dutchman didn't press him further on the topic. He talked about his subsequent plunge into the bottle, which Van Wyk knew only too well himself. Soon, Van Wyk came to understand the pain that had brought Tom to this juncture and how Heidi filled a void vacated by his lost child. He knew he would soon have to abandon his own child, and his heart ached for the loss she would endure. But he began to wonder if he might not be able to help them both.

Heidi's father explained to Tom that he was a Nederlander whose family had come from Assen in northeast Netherlands via Hamburg, Germany, to South Africa in 1890 when he was ten. This made him only forty-two, although he looked years older. His eyes lit up, speaking of his childhood on a small farm, the dance festivals, and the local market. He was clearly a man of the land. He had settled in Northern Rhodesia on a homestead with his parents and older brother. But his life had been full of tragedy, too. His brother, who was ten years his senior, was killed in the Boer War, and his parents died shortly thereafter, leaving him to manage the farm alone. He, too, had also lost his wife, Heidi's mother, to scarlet fever five years before. He recently moved to Cape Town, he explained, so that he could be close to a good hospital as his disease progressed and so that Heidi could go to school. He always stopped short of discussing his daughter's future. Instead, he would silence Tom and change the subject, insisting that he did not wish to discuss it. Tom admired his strength and desire to keep things as normal for the child as possible, but it irked him that he refused to plan for Heidi's future and provide any arrangements for her care after his demise. He wondered if the Children's Home here in Cape Town had really been the impetus for their move and if that was his ultimate plan- to place her in the orphanage upon his death. But the conversation was never allowed to meander into that territory.

One particularly rainy Sunday morning, Heidi was eating breakfast downstairs with Tom and Weasel. Tom noted a sense of worry when Heidi came down alone, claiming that Papa was not feeling too well and preferred to sleep. Weasel and Tom exchanged looks, and Tom insisted that Weasel engage Heidi in a game of checkers after breakfast so he could check in on her father. Tom let himself into his room to find Van Wyk looking particularly frail. He was sitting up in bed, reading his bible. His eyes were weary and strained. He had been hitting the whiskey hard already. The pain must have been unbearable. He felt such empathy for this man who had no choice about living or dying: the choice had been made for him. He sat gently next to him on the bed, and Van Wyk lifted his eyes from the page.

"I'm not here to talk about me, Charles," said Tom resolutely. This was new, as both men typically formally addressed each other when conversing.

"You aren't getting better…you know that. Have you thought about your daughter's future?"

"I am well aware of my condition Mr. Sutton." Van Wyk responded unyieldingly.

"Have you told her?"

"Yes, everything, Mr. Sutton. She knows that she will not have my hand to hold soon. I have prepared my daughter for that spiteful day myself." Swallowing the lump in his throat, the Dutchman continued. "I might not leave behind a fortune for my daughter, but what I still own, a thousand miles away, with the right help and guidance, will be hers when she is of age, and it will provide adequately for her future."

Tom stared at him in wonderment. He had had no idea that Heidi was so aware, and he admired his strength of conviction. The Dutchman continued.

"What I am leaving behind for her is the truth. I made sure to tell my daughter what will happen in the coming days, so she will be equipped with moral strength to deal with her current situation." he closed his bible and laid it in his lap. "My daughter loves me to the furthest corner of the world, and I love her too, of course. But it worries me sick. I am all that she has. She may be young, but as you know, she is clever beyond her years, and she understands that this disease has no alternative ending. She understands that she will have no one to rely on except herself when I am gone, as we have no relatives here, and this land is all she knows. I have assured my daughter that the only thing that leaves an imprint forever, a legacy that outlives age, sickness, and death, is love. I have taught her how to share her love for life with all those around her, regardless of race, language, status, or state of mind." He nodded to Tom, indicating he was the latter.

"Her love for life and the people she meets in it will serve her well. She is not to waste her days crying for me, for I will always remain with her in her heart, and she knows that. And if she trusts in God and adheres to my lessons, she will never truly find herself an orphan…she will never truly be alone."

Both men sat in silence, and without a word spoken, their tears flowed freely. Van Wyk wept for the child he would soon lose and Tom for the memory of one already lost. Van Wyk had never been a soldier but had the heart of the mightiest warrior, thought Tom. Somehow, Van Wyk and Heidi were at peace with the drastic plunge their life was about to take, while Tom saw himself only picking at his open wound.

Wiping his tears with a handkerchief, Van Wyk poured himself another glass of whiskey from the bottle on his side drawer and drank it down to the rising lump in his throat. Tom wiped his tears with the corner of his thumb. Steadying his voice, the Dutchman looked at Tom with glassy eyes and hinted ever so subtly.

"Perhaps, Thomas, you can visit my daughter when she is moved into the orphanage? Van Wyk would never ask. He had hoped that Tom had grown to love his daughter enough. But he was a proud man and wouldn't beg. He simply added, "She will need a friend… someone connecting her to her past."

"Of course, I will as long as life permits me to," Tom affirmed.

Tom wanted to tell the Dutchman how he caught a glimpse of Sean every time Heidi smiled. He desperately wanted to tell him how he could raise Heidi as his daughter and care for her. He knew an orphanage was no place for this child and that no matter how strong her moral courage was, it would damage her. His son would never know him, but he longed to assure Van Wyk that he would keep his memory alive for Heidi so she would never forget him. He wanted to reach out for Van Wyk's hand and solicit his permission to turn Heidi to his care, but Tom had failed his own family, and Van Wyk probably thought him unworthy. The words dissolved in Tom's throat.

After a moment, Van Wyk smiled in appreciation and expressed his gratitude to Tom for his friendship and promise to visit Heidi in the orphanage. He had great hope that when the moment presented itself, Tom would consider adopting Heidi, but he realized that was a great expectation. He had come to know Sutton well over the past two months, and he was convinced that he could care for Heidi and love her like his own. He also knew that the void that gnawed at

Tom's heart might be healed by his brave little daughter. He had sincerely hoped that Tom would see it, too.

The awkwardness was disrupted as Heidi busted through the door, singing with a tray full of food for her father. Van Wyk straightened up in bed and smoothed down his hair. As Heidi placed the tray down in front of him, he grabbed her hand and gave it a kiss, and she curtsied. They all laughed.

Tom rose as Heidi took his place on the bed beside her father. She chattered on about how she had beaten Weasel fair and square and that she was going to be the checkers champion of Cape Town. Lying in her father's lap, Van Wyk stroked her golden hair as he looked up at Sutton with sad eyes.

"Papa, if you aren't well enough to come to dinner can I have dinner with Mr. Tom," Heidi asked, staring up at Tom, smiling. "I want to beat him at the next game of checkers."

"You can call him Uncle Tom if he is fine with it," said Van Wyk, searching for Tom's approval

Tom nodded in return and held his hand out for Heidi, who reached for it. He bowed and then grabbed her other hand and spun her around her circles as she laughed and laughed. Each time he plopped her back on her feet, she screamed, "oh again, Uncle Tom again … please," and the spinning resumed until they both collapsed on the floor, dizzy with laughter. Van Wyk fought back the tears with a smile as he watched them together. Heidi was so full of life and potential, and Tom could teach his daughter to spread her wings. Why could he not see what a pair they made?

In the days and weeks that followed, Van Wyk got weaker and was now mostly confined to his bed. He had resolved himself to the orphanage and had made necessary arrangements, but he encouraged Heidi to spend as much time with Uncle Tom as she wished. He hoped it would continue to tighten their bond and, at the very least, offer Heidi a chance to laugh and enjoy her childhood during these dark days.

Tom easily fell back into the role of father. Tom and Heidi would spend their weekends outdoors. They both loved the fresh air and sunshine on their faces and could often be found building sandcastles at the beach. They even got Weasel in on the act, fetching them buckets of water for the castle moat as he complained about the hot sun searing his delicate Irish skin.

Tom taught Heidi how to swim, and they would spend hours chasing each other through the waves. It reminded Tom of the lake in Lough Tay, and that made him happy. Hide and seek in the boarding house was another favorite pastime until Mrs. Baldwin caught Tom hiding in the broom closet and gave him a piece of her mind. Heidi's father enjoyed the animated retelling of how the landlady berated Uncle Tom. Mrs. Baldwin found the new cheery Tom to be more of a nuisance than the old drunk version, but she too kept her silence like Weasel most of the time, for Heidi's sake. Even with her generally disagreeable disposition, she had come to like the little girl, who was always willing to help around the boarding house, asking for nothing in return. She was grateful that Heidi had finally found a caring friend while her father wasted away in the room upstairs.

Everyone came to see Heidi and Tom as a pair. If you didn't know their background, one would assume they were family since they had an ease and affection for each other, like father and daughter. Weasel was the only sceptic. He cared for Heidi, too and recognized the fragile situation within which she lived, but he was afraid this new friendship would come at a hefty cost. Tom acted like her father, and he became fearful of how vulnerable he might be when this all came to an end. Tom might have recovered once from a terrible heartache, but he wasn't sure Tom could sustain another. Weasel was afraid his friend would forfeit his again on life again, and he needed him.

One Sunday morning after breakfast, Tom and Heidi were sprawled on the carpet in the parlor, playing their usual Sunday checkers tournament. Weasel sat smoking in the armchair in the corner of the room, reading the paper and chuckling to see Heidi beat Tom solidly again. Tom never intentionally let Heidi win, and that made it even funnier. She was a serious contender even at her young age.

"The little child is winning again," said Weasel sarcastically. "My papa taught me how to play with strategy. Back on our farm, we used to play checkers every night after dinner," Heidi looked up to respond to Weasel's comments while grinning.

"Farm? - you never told me that you lived on a farm, Heidi," said Weasel folding the paper.

"Oh yes, my father has a big farm. The best in all Northern Rhodesia. It makes me sad sometimes that I may never be able to see it again."

"Why can't you, Heidi?" Weasel asked, unable to prevent the words from coming out. Tom shook his head disapprovingly.

"Because Papa is too sick now, Uncle Timothy. When he goes to heaven, I will be going to the orphanage."

She stared at them both with watery blue eyes. Tom quickly changed the subject.

"So, my little Heidi, what quest shall we embark on today?" "How about swimming, Uncle Tom? Please, please, can we go to the beach?"

"And our tournament?"

"We can finish it once we return, Uncle Tom, please?"

Tom's rigid posture relaxed, watching how fast Heidi's spirit elevated. He smiled to himself…Sean used to do the same thing.

"I admit defeat," he said, throwing his hands in the air dramatically.

"Defeat, Uncle Tom?"

"That means you won, Heidi. Uncle Tom is no match for the expert. Go get your things, and we'll go to the beach."

"What about you, Uncle Timothy? Will you be joining us?" "Why would I want to go to the bloody…?"

"Language, Uncle Timothy," Heidi scolded the grown men, making him and Tom laugh at her antics.

"You know, Heidi, how much I dislike washing my face. Then, why would I willingly bask in the undertows of the Atlantic and Indian Oceans?"

Heidi laughed at Weasel and hummed her way up the stairs to get changed. When her soft hums were no longer audible, Weasel crossed to Tom, adjusting his sinking trousers and muttering under his breath how it would be a miracle the day he found trousers to fit him.

He lit another one of his cigarettes and puffed it methodically through the open window, watching the smoke escape in little clouds. Tom knew what Weasel was brooding.

"You haven't told her yet, have you?" "No," said Tom angrily

"Why not, Tom? You should not be raising her hopes like Cape Rollers. We are leaving in less than two weeks. For Christ's sake, Tom."

"What do you want me to tell her, Weasel? That I won't be here anymore, acting as her father, while her own father dies upstairs?"

"Tell her whatever you want, Tom. You can comfort her with a lie, but she's a smart lass. She'll understand if you tell her that you got a decent job in a mine, putting your skills to use. Just explain to her that just like her father is a farmer, this is your skillset, and you must go where the work is. She will understand. That kid has more intelligence than the two of us combined."

Weasel didn't want to create a rift between them. But he was angry that Tom had led her on for the past two weeks. He was making this parting worse for everyone involved.

Tom acquiesced. He couldn't hurt Weasel, who had stood by him through thick and thin, so he asked Weasel for the address of their new lodging so he could share it with Heidi if she ever wished to write to them.

"Of course, give her the address. Hopefully, it's better than this hellhole of Baldwin's. Maybe if she still remembers us, she'll write. Or maybe she will move on."

Ignoring the rage in his tone, he promised Weasel he would come clean and tell the Van Wyk of their plans. Just then, Heidi arrived in her swimming costume and beach hat. Weasel forced a smile and excused himself.

Weasel recognized that Heidi had saved his friend from a life of misery and drunkenness, but he had spent two years making just enough money to keep a roof above their heads. Now that Tom was clear of his mind, it was time for them to move on. This Southern

Rhodesian mining contract was their way out. They could not stay locked up here, barely surviving. And besides, this little girl deserved a future far more secure than anything they could provide her. Weasel figured that Tom had been an orphan, and he turned out alright. Her father had left her a little farm or something…surely when she was old enough to leave the orphanage, she would assume her inheritance, and that would provide enough for her future. She would probably end up marrying a Dutch farmer, and Tom would become a distant memory. Weasel rationalized everything into a tidy little compartment in his mind.

The sun was hot, and Tom shielded his eyes with his hand as Heidi tugged at his other hand, trying to pull him up out of his trance and to the water. Tom jolted forward, and Heidi tumbled back onto the sand, giggling. He pulled her up to her feet and went down on his knees to meet her face to face, her little hands in his, all full of sand.

"Heidi, I have something to tell you."

"What is it, Uncle Tom? Is it a surprise? Oh, you give the best surprises, Uncle Tom!"

Heidi smiled as her eyes were filled with expectation. His heart broke under the weight of what he had to say. Clearing his throat, he told her it was not the surprise she wanted to hear.

CHAPTER 11

Simalala

"So, I see you have grown to enjoy submerging yourself, have you, Mr. Byrne?" Tom mocked Weasel as his skinny frame crawled, dripping out of a large tin bathtub on the far side of their shared hut.

Weasel didn't hold back his annoyance. "Not my fault. This place is fecking' dusty, mate."

The two grown men had relinquished their reasonably modern accommodations at the city boarding house for a native thatched hut constructed with wattle and daub. But Tom didn't care about comfort. This hut was private and simple. They had a small kitchen set up in the back area of the hut with some basic supplies and utensils, although most of their meals were taken outside under the stars around a campfire. Tom leaned back in his chair, amused, as he sat puffing a cigar at the two-person folding kitchen table. Next to the kitchen area, two army-style cots were set side by side, with a small table in between with a lantern and box of matches. They were comfortable. In the bathroom area, close to the front door, stood Weasel, now jumping on one foot, trying to get the water out of his ear.

The bathroom, if you could call it that, consisted of a wash bowl and jug, two hooks for towels, a small table for soap, a comb, some shaving accoutrements, and, of course, the tin bathtub that they had lobbied the boss to pick up for them. There was no indoor plumbing, but the outhouse was only twenty or so feet from the exterior of the dwelling, along with a good pump.

In their spare time, they had painted the interior of the hut white and hung vibrant orange curtains on the two small glass-paned windows, courtesy of one of Weasel's shopping trips to Bulawayo. Over the last few years living with Weasel, Tom had learned to accept his eccentric color selection. After all, the decorating had never been up to him anyway. Tom liked how uncomplicated this place was, and it was oddly reminiscent of the Gallaghers' cottage in Lough Tay.

"'Tis my family cottage; Tom and I shall decorate it how I see fit," he remembered her saying with a sigh and half a smile.

He was doing better these days. The mining work wasn't bad. At least he was using some of his old "skills," he thought. He liked that element of danger. The adrenaline rush kept him feeling alive.

The hut was the property of their new employer, an old Swedish pioneer that Tom and Weasel surmised was probably in his sixties, although he had not weathered well. Gold was first discovered in Mthwakazi in 1867, and white settlers began arriving in droves by the end of the century.

The Swede first set foot on this foreign land in 1893, a mere four years after Cecil Rhodes. Rhodes, a British businessman and staunch believer in British Imperialism, secured a Royal charter to form the British South Africa Company, giving him exclusive mineral rights to the region. Like Rhodes, the Swede was an adventurer at heart. He had befriended the local inhabitants upon his arrival, and after a year of living among them, a Shona native led him to the site of an ancient mine in Southern Matabeleland.

With no desire for a wife and family, he was content with a solo life of gold prospecting and had built a small house for himself near the mine, committing himself to a life in the bush. He was industrious and amiable and made friends with the local Ndebele, learning native survival tricks while employing some of them in his mine. From 1893 to 1896, he endured the turbulence of the Matabele War between the British South Africa Company and the Ndebele and Shona. He kept his head down and stayed far from the fray and the politics, choosing to remain with his mine among the natives until the Matabele ultimately lost to the superior firepower of the British.

In 1895, Matabeleland, which consisted of North Matabeleland, South Matabeleland, and Bulawayo, was divided into plots and sold for high prices to white pioneer prospectors flooding the area. At that time, the Swede secured a proper claim to the small mine and endeavored to stay indefinitely. The region then became known as Rhodesia, the North and South being split by the Zambezi River. This year, he had seen the British crown finally claim Southern Rhodesia and the British South Africa Company cede its mineral rights to the territory for two million pounds.

He was a friendly sort, yet shrewd and somewhat paranoid. He rarely hired white mine workers, but Weasel had convinced him of their expertise and trustworthiness. He had responded to this advertisement, citing their experience fighting for Irish liberation and their extensive work with explosives. The Swede had no love for the British, and these Irishmen seemed trustworthy enough. So far, they have proved to be hard workers.

Tom had no idea what Weasel had divulged in that letter to the Swede to get them this job, and he was satisfied not knowing. He liked the Swede. He didn't ask a lot of questions. The mine was insignificant in size, and no one really knew the precise profit the Swede was yielding from it, and again, Tom was convinced it was for the best. He was never showy or extravagant, and he did all the accounting himself. He kept his safe secure, with the key notably hidden and never seen in the light of day. He had a small office attached to his modest whitewashed house, Dutch style, about a five-minute walk from their hut, which was right next to the mine itself.

Occasionally, he would invite Tom and Weasel over for a scotch, his drink of choice, and a cigar, the latter of which Weasel abhorred. Considering they weren't professional miners, Tom and Weasel were offered a handsome amount. This only confirmed Tom's suspicion that the old man was wary of hiring any professional white gold miner for fear of being swindled.

The Swede was an experienced local guide who spoke Shona fluently and was comfortable in the bush. He was also very well-versed when it came to mining and, specifically, his claim. He would run through intricate drawings of the mine with his workers and knew exactly where to order Sutton to blast a specific vein for gold.

"Blast this open to perfection, Irish." he'd say with an authority he had undoubtedly earned. Tom knew that the old man would rather do it himself but was astute enough to recognize that he was too frail to outrun the fuse on the dynamite.

Life had become comfortably mundane for Sutton, who followed the Swede's orders for the last few months and saved all his wages for some future adventure he had yet to uncover. The monotony was punctured every month or so with a trip to Bulawayo, about forty miles from the mine. The occasion allowed the Swede to weigh and bank the fruits of his labor while Tom and Weasel picked up supplies and dropped or picked up letters from the post office. Tom had continued to write to Heidi and him to her. She didn't see unhappy, but her letters lacked that spark, that sheer joy he had come to associate with her. With every letter, guilt tugged at his heart a little, but they were leading to separate lives, and he couldn't see a way around that.

Tom had been happier in his last few weeks in Cape Town. He often thought of Heidi and her father, Charles, and despite the ease of this new life, he knew it wouldn't be forever.

Conversely, Weasel, as Tom's designated assistant, was enjoying a feeling of self-importance. And given that this job was far less strenuous than hauling crates all day, he found the work somewhat recreational and perceived himself to be a valuable asset to the mine's daily operation. He had also developed a rapport amongst the African laborers and soon realized his status and the color of his skin allowed him to dictate orders and play the role of the supervisor in a way he had never done before. Their lives were stable here, and although he knew that Tom missed Heidi or simply the idea of being a father again, he believed this situation was better for him.

"Filth and water together conceive treasures." sputtered Weasel, shaking the bathwater free from his unruly mop of hair. This has clearly been a trial for him from beginning to end. Tom chuckled as Weasel sauntered over to the table, wearing only his towel around his waist. He proceeded to flop down on one of the two chairs at their kitchen table in exasperation.

"What are your plans for tonight?" said Tom. "Now that you're as clean and fresh as a daisy?"

"I might go to see Molly," said Weasel under his breath

Tom took another pull of the cigar and coughed slightly. "The farm's a bit too close for my comfort. Someday, that old Boer farmer might come here to blow out your brains for fooling around with his sybaritic daughter."

Embarrassed at the suggestion that she might only be using him, he quickly diverted his attention to the cloud of cigar smoke that now overwhelmed the space between them.

"For Christ's sake, you're smooching those heinous sticks again? They reek more than a rotten cabbage," Weasel exclaimed, dramatically wafting the smoke away from his face. "I'll never forgive the Swede for turning you on to those bloody things."

"This is your fate now, Weasel. Best that you embrace it. Like you, I have accepted the finest offerings of life." Tom declared with a wink and released a thick smoke ring in Weasel's direction.

"Bejesus, thank the Lord, you don't smoke them underground. That's the only place I can get away from the bloody things. I would rather breathe in the sweat of half a dozen men in the mine instead of that bloody thing."

Weasel rushed to the front door and swung it open, unable to withstand the cigar cloud invading every crevice of the room. And standing in nothing but a towel, rhythmically waved the smoke out of the hut.

The scene of this scrawny, almost naked Irishman dancing like an imp with his hands flailing from side to side brought Tom to his knees in laughter until tears erupted down his face. Tom's roaring laughter only aggravated Weasel more as he shouted obscenities at Tom. Gravity finally got the best of him, and his towel lost its grip and fell limp on the floor, making him kick it out in front of him, exasperated.

Tom's ensuing laughter was cut off swiftly when he saw Simalala running full speed towards the hut. Turning to see the African approaching, Weasel reached for his discarded towel and quickly wrapped it back around his waist. Abruptly extinguishing his cigar, Tom rushed out the door to meet Simalala, who was visibly panting as he neared the hut.

Simalala was a six-foot tall, athletic black man in his mid-thirties, originally from Barotseland. He had short, tight hair, a wide brow, and kind dark brown eyes. He wore a pair of khaki work pants with no shirt. He had become the Swede's assistant some ten years earlier, and the old man held him in high regard. Tom took note of the man's clenched muscles as he bent over, gripping his knees for support and panting to catch his breath.

"Bwana."

"Everything all right, Simalala?"

"Bwana Swede look for you, Bwana Tom. Trouble sometimes." said Simalala between breaths.

"Take a deep breath," said Tom, waiting for him to regulate his breathing.

"What happened, Simalala? What's the trouble?" said Tom nervously.

"Mine… cave in," uttered Simalala, full of fear.

This was one thing all miners feared. What the hell was the Swede doing so far? Thought Tom. And why was he now responsible for the rescue? A thousand emotions raked through Tom's mind in seconds. He wasn't a miner. He didn't know the first thing about rescuing someone from a mine cave-in. Now, he'd have to put his life and Weasel's in jeopardy to try and save a man he barely knew. It was a gamble, a gamble with his own life.

"Bwana, you come now?" "There are twenty-five in there."

Tom closed his eyes and took a deep breath before affirming his help, "I come now, Simalala."

On cue, Weasel barged out of the hut dressed in his union suit and a haplessly pulled-on pair of dirty breeches. Seeing Tom lay his hand on Simalala's shoulder, he knew something bad had happened.

"What's happening, Thomas?"

"The mine collapsed; 25 men are trapped in." "How the bloody hell did that happen?"

"We'll find out after we get there." "Just my luck, eh?"

"Your luck to be a savior?"

"No! My bloody luck. I just had a bath!

CHAPTER 12

The Gold Mine

When Tom and Weasel arrived at the scene of the catastrophe with Simalala, two rugged African men with solemn expressions stood guard over the windlass while several other laborers stood nearby talking nervously. The two men had been tasked with guarding the windlass and the shaft. They were to operate the crank and lower anything essential for the rescue, per Tom's instructions. The air was thick and humid, and the fear was palpable on everyone's faces. A small wooden platform was attached to the thick rope that wound around the winch. The platform had been raised and was awaiting their instructions.

"Where is Bwana Swede?" Tom asked, glancing nervously down at the seemingly bottomless narrow recess.

"Panzi"[1]

Wasting no time, Tom climbed onto the platform and had the men lower him down into the shaft. He instructed them to pull the platform back up upon his signal and await further instructions. The Africans were swift in reciprocating the orders, well aware of the delicacy of the situation. Clutching his carbide lamp close to him, Tom mumbled a quick prayer as the walls of the shaft became narrower as

---

[1] Down.

he descended, and the thoughts of cobras tucked in the holes of this cave sent a shiver down his spine.

He did not enjoy being underground in Africa. He would take a sewer rat under the Dublin City streets any day over a snake slithering from a hole in the rock. Nearly eighty feet underground now, he glanced upwards for a moment as the halo of distant daylight almost disappeared from view. Once his ride touched the ground with a slight jerk, he tugged at the rope thrice, signaling for the platform to be pulled back to the surface. Tom took a deep, uneasy breath as he felt the dank atmosphere of the once familiar tunnel turn foreboding.

Tom couldn't walk upright in this tunnel and had to crouch as he made his way forward. The tunnel was barely five feet, six inches high, and a mere three feet wide. Typically, claustrophobia didn't bother him, but today, the tunnel felt dangerous and unpredictable. Approaching the first station, the space widened, and he observed the figure of the old man, lamp in hand and covered in dust, looking like a ghost sitting dejectedly on an empty bucket. He recognized his beard and familiar posture in the lamplight and called out.

"Why are you sitting down here, for God's sake… it's dangerous?" "Are you alright?"

The Swede shrugged off Tom's question with a word and merely stood, raised his lamp, and beckoned him to follow as he led the way towards the second station. It wasn't until they approached the second station that he turned and,

looking Sutton earnestly in the face, said, "Thank you for coming, Irish."

The duo stepped into the clearing of station two, where four tunnels diverged. Each was only wide enough for a man to crawl through on all fours. The entrance to the third tunnel was almost completely clogged with rocks and debris.

Creasing his forehead in worry, Tom said in a whisper. "So, they are in there? "How did this happen?"

"This tunnel…I call it Irish after you because you blasted it and collapsed when they were returning with rocks. Not your fault, of course. Two dead confirmed. Some got out, but some are still trapped in there."

"How many are trapped? Do you know?" "Twelve."

"Twelve? But Simalala said twenty-five."

"It was such a disaster when it happened. You couldn't even see a foot in front of you. Twenty-five minutes were initially down here with me, so when it collapsed, that was my best guess. After I sent him for help, I started pulling rocks from the entrance until I heard voices. I was able to remove enough to fashion a big enough hole to crawl through, and almost half of them managed to scramble out."

"So, what makes you so certain that the remaining twelve are trapped and not dead?" said Tom

"I'm not completely certain they are all alive, but I'm guessing that the tunnel must have collapsed in segments. After I got the first lot of lucky bastards out, I crawled into the tunnel as far as I could go, and I could hear them on the other side of the rubble. Some, I imagine, are badly hurt, but they are alive -all except the two that were furthest in, like I said before. They didn't make it. Irish, look, these are my caves, and I make sure that each tunnel has an air tunnel for ventilation. Those men have no food or water, but they can breathe for now. But we don't have much time, and I worry that the air tunnel won't last."

Since Tom really was an amateur in this mining operation, he asked the Swede if he had any ideas for a rescue mission.

"We cannot blast. It will cave in the whole mine. We have to go underground."

"Underground? What do you mean?"

"A happy mistake. When we were working in the direction of a new feeder reef and digging this tunnel, one of the young ones was digging a new tunnel in the wrong direction and didn't know it was the same reef we were already working on. It's not big, but it goes right beneath tunnel three. If that mistake can save these men now, I'll make him my boss boy."

"Then let's get on with it," Tom affirmed and motioned for the Swede to lead the way since he wasn't fond of exchanging words unnecessarily, and time was precious. They stood outside the fourth narrow tunnel that the young African had been working on, and Tom held up his lamp and could see how the tunnel sloped downwards and to the right.

"This is it. The men are trapped about twenty-five or thirty feet in tunnel three. Based on the thirty-degree downward slope of this tunnel, I calculate that when you are twenty-five feet in, you will be about fifteen feet below tunnel three, almost directly under them, give or take. You'll have to dig up fifteen feet to get to them Irish. It's pretty hopeless, but it's all we have."

Tom processed the information quickly, making the same mental calculations, and nodded in affirmation. When they arrived back at station one, they were met with an array of concerned faces in the clearing awaiting instructions.

"What the hell are you all doing here?" Tom barked

"They came to help their brothers in need," Weasel replied on behalf of all the African laborers. The men all nodded in agreement.

Tom's restrained shoulders loosened. "They can do so by staying up there and praying," he said earnestly, as his mind was already working overtime.

"So, can you help Irish?" muttered the Swede in half disbelief "I can try," Tom said, dusting off his hands and throwing Weasel a knowing glance. "What do you need?"

"Two picks, more carbide lamps, dust masks, a twenty-five-foot length of rope, and a worthy volunteer."

"And that is my cue," Weasel announced, stepping to the front from the little crowd that had formed in the tunnel.

"Oh no, not you, Weasel. No offence, my friend, but I need a volunteer who can do some damage with a pick and sustain lifting hundreds of pounds of rocks for the next, however many hours it may take. And besides, I am putting everyone in your charge. Please get these people out of here and give us room to work, including the boss." Even the Swede nodded and acquiesced, knowing that there was little he could do underground to aid the rescue.

Weasel knew not to argue with Sutton and that when the time came, he would call on him for what was necessary. Tom was in his element. Making plans and executing them in difficult circumstances was his strong suit, and the adrenaline only made him better. Before leaving Tom, the Swede gave him an encouraging pat on the shoulder.

"I'll be waiting for you to return with my workers, Irish. I am too old now, and I don't think I can train any more boys."

As the Swede ascended the windlass and disappeared up the shaft, Tom addressed the men, some of whom were merely boys no older than sixteen or seventeen. They reminded him of young Patrick. He hated subjecting youngsters to danger beyond their years.

"I need one strong volunteer?" he sighed deeply.

Thankfully, Simalala stepped from the crowd to render his service to Tom, and the others nodded in agreement, praising the man that they had all come to respect.

"The work is scary, brave one. Are you sure?" Tom said honestly.

"Simalala, no scare, Bwana Tom." retorted the man without a wince.

Tom offered the dauntless man a smile and a pat on the shoulder in return for his display of courage. After the others had ascended and Tom's requested equipment had arrived, he and Simalala made their way to the fourth tunnel in station two. Tom ventured on all fours once again into the darkness with Simalala right behind him, leaving a lamp at the entrance and the end of the twenty-five-foot rope, allowing it to unravel to the right length as they moved forward. As they descended down the sloping tunnel, Tom held the carbide lamp ahead of them to light their way, followed by Simalala, who dragged along their masks and picked behind him. As the silence started creeping in, Tom broke it to keep any doubts from prevailing.

"Why do you call me Bwana and not Nkosi like the others?"
"Because I am not Ndebele. Where I come from, Bwana is for white men like you."

"You are not from here?"

"No. I come from Barotseland. Five hundred miles away, the white men say."

"Where the hell is that?"

"Far away. Mosi-oa-Tunya, where the great waterfall of Zambezi is. Abelungu[2] calls it Victoria Falls, where the smoke thunders. That is my home. I will go back to my Umfazis[3] and Piccanins[4] soon after I have enough money."

As he continued to make mental calculations with each push forward, Tom's mind drifted to Heidi. Hearing that Simalala was from Northern Rhodesia made him wonder what had happened to Van Wyk's farm, if Heidi was in, and if she would ever return to her home.

The tunnel was suffocating and desolate. It was so quiet; it was hard to believe that any life existed anywhere close to them. The duo kept crawling further into the darkness. Tom hoped the Swede's calculations and his assumptions were accurate, or they would be digging in vain. As they reached the end of the rope, Tom mustered the most confident voice he could, not only for Simalala's benefit but for his own, too, and affirmed that they had arrived.

"Here is where we start digging, Simalala."

Even though they could barely sit without their heads scraping the top of the tunnel, they raised their picks and wasted no time hurling jabs at the earth above them. After an hour of swinging their picks back and forth without a word spoken between them, they noticed how little progress they had actually made. Given their uncompromising position, crouched on their knees, and restricted movement in the tunnel, they had only managed to create an indent about a foot deep while polluting the air around them with thick dust. Tom knew they were far from reaching tunnel three, and at this pace, they would lose their race against time or the strength to keep digging.

Simalala was clearly under a similar assumption and asked Tom how much further they had to dig. Tom remained silent because he knew that this was hopeless, and he was mulling something else over in his mind. Maneuvering around Simalala towards the exit, he simply said.

---

[2]   White People
[3]   Wives
[4]   Children

"Keep digging, Simalala. I will be back shortly." "Where you go, Bwana Tom?"

"I'll be quick. I have a better idea than this."

As Tom returned to station two, his lamp illuminated Weasel's distressed visage entering the tunnel.

"What the bloody hell did you think you were doing?" "Coming to get you and Simalala out of here."

"Why the hell would you do that?"

"Because the Swede thinks the air tunnel has crashed. We assumed you couldn't hear the rumble. He told me to come down here and get you out."

"Shit! I'll be damned. I should have gone with my plan in the first place."

"What plan, Thomas?" "To blast an opening."

Weasel's eyes bulged out of their sockets in bewilderment at the suggestion.

"You're a fucking madman, Sutton. Not only will you kill yourself, but the Swede won't allow it."

"Only if he finds out, my friend. So, will you keep your mouth shut and get me the supplies, Weasel?"

"And just why the bloody hell would I help you orchestrate your own death, especially after everything we've been through?"

"Just shut up and get me the dynamite."

Tom shoved Weasel back towards the second station. He wasn't taking no for an answer. Weasel scrambled back up to the station, contemplating that despite how dangerous this idea was, they really had no other option. Twelve men would surely die if they did nothing, and even though he had faith in Sutton's instincts, this was the first time he'd hatched a plan with little substantive planning. With no alternatives, Weasel made a reappearance fifteen minutes later in the tunnel with a sack of a dozen dynamite sticks.

"I know… I am the bees' knees." grinned Weasel uneasily. "How did you get past the Swede?"

"I told him Simalala was hurt and needed a stretcher. While he was getting the stretcher and medical supplies together, I escaped back down here with these. It better be worth his wrath, Sutton."

"It will be if we empty three-quarters of the powder out of these. Eight should do it."

After the dynamite sticks were prepped, Weasel handed him a box of matches, and Tom ran through the plan again with Weasel, just like old times. Cautiously optimistic, Weasel headed back to the windlass to head off the Swede and any others who he anticipated might be on their way down to help. Tom crawled his way back down the tunnel to Simalala.

"I thought you left me. Work is hard." smiled Simalala amiably as sweat dripped from his temples and down his back. He was glad to see his face.

"It will get harder, my friend. The men trapped have lost their air tunnel." Tom said solemnly.

Simalala immediately understood the danger and listened carefully as Tom explained the new rescue plan. The two men worked quickly to dig eight holes fifteen inches apart and placed the sticks strategically. Once the task was complete, Tom convinced Simalala begrudgingly to make his way out to the station, where he would join him as soon as the dynamite sticks were lit. Tom waited until he could no longer see the back of Simalala before he struck the match and began lighting sticks.

As Tom scrambled out of the opening of the tunnel, a cacophonous blast rattled the area around them, and the crawl space behind him became engulfed in earth and debris. Simalala and Tom coughed, gasped for clean air, and could barely see each other's faces. Thankfully, Weasel had been true to his word, and the station appeared to be empty. So, only Simalala, Tom, and twelve trapped men remained in this dust-filled cave.

Tom anxiously waited for the dust to settle so he could get a better look at the tunnel and their handiwork. They exchanged a hopeful, bloodshot look and, still coughing, crawled back into the tunnel to take note, rummaging through the rocks like rabid dogs.

The debris was loose and easy to move, and with Simalala's strength, they quickly removed the rocks and funneled their way back to the site of the blast. The nearly two feet they had managed to dig in the past hour and a half had expanded. Another had ten feet at least, thanks to the dynamite. Tom grinned at the sight before him and patted Simalala on the back, who exchanged the same look of exuberance. They could now easily stand in the space and set to work with ebullience to tackle the remaining three feet.

They took their turns to aim at the earth, disregarding the scrapes and bruises on their bodies as gravel and rock pummeled them from above. They were very close. Tom could feel it, and taking one last mighty swing at what he perceived to be the last few inches, a massive chunk of rock and debris broke off, crushing him underneath. Only a couple of feet from the heap, Simalala stood petrified and released a guttural cry to the empty cave.

Abandoning his pick, Simalala crawled over the heap to see that Tom was still breathing and appeared alert, but his chest and arm were besieged under the heavy rubble. He wrestled with the rocks to free the trapped man. The veins in his arms bulged as he pushed his muscles to their limit. As he worked to remove the rock, Simalala watched the pain and agony etched on Tom's face morph into an expression of sheer joy. Turning, he looked up to see two grinning, dusty black faces peering back at him from the hole above them. Sutton then slipped into oblivion.

Soon, the tunnel behind him was filled with helpers. After the blast, Weasel had made his way back down with a few of the men, and after hearing Simalala call out, they had worked fast to carve out the tunnel, removing more debris and creating a wider escape route. Seeing them, Simalala collapsed on the heap in thankful exhaustion as the other group of men took over, removing the rubble off Tom and helping the men down through the hole. However unconventional, the rescue had been a success, and Tom Sutton was damaged but alive.

CHAPTER 13

A Hospital Stay

Tom's heroism did not go unrewarded. The Swede, immensely grateful for the rescue of his men, spared no expense for Tom's medical treatment and convalescence. He insisted that they travel to Johannesburg so Tom could receive expert care at the General Hospital. There, he underwent surgery for a broken arm and was treated for a concussion, fractured ribs, and other scrapes and bruises.

Weasel, who was to accompany his friend and stay with him until he fully recovered, was set up with fine accommodations at the Grand Station Hotel, a welcome change from their mining hut, even for Weasel.

Tom's condition was quite serious for the first two days of his hospital stay. His surgery had gone well, and his other physical wounds were not life-threatening. His recovery should have been swift, but he continued to slip in and out of consciousness, which concerned his doctor. Dr. Gerhardt was a brooding sort. The stocky German physician sported a well-groomed moustache and a wrinkled forehead full of consternation. He was all business.

"Mr. Sutton is still obviously suffering from a concussion. His fractured arm and bruised ribs will take some time to heal, but they are not my concern, Mr. Byrne," said Dr Gerhardt as the two looked through the window into Tom's room, where he lay motionless in his hospital bed.

"Your friend is not in a coma, Mr. Byrne, but he does seem to lapse into a semi-conscious state quite often. I have listened to him. He misses his family, perhaps. He calls out for them and then slips back into a deep sleep like he is unconscious.

Sometimes, he can even be responsive to his surroundings when he is in one of his lucid moments, and then he is gone again. He seems to be asking for Grace and Sean, and sometimes he asks for Heidi. Mr. Byrne, do you know who any of these people are, and can you contact them and have them come to him? I do believe it may speed up the healing process. It would be of great help to Mr. Sutton."

Weasel looked at his friend through the glass, tucked in like a child, in the sterile white sheets. Despite the successful rescue operation, he felt oddly responsible. He was decidedly useless at thwarting Tom when he was on a mission. He turned to face the man in the white coat and, choking back a lump in his throat, enlightened the doctor, who listened carefully.

"Grace and Sean were his families back in Ireland: His wife and his son. But they aren't alive anymore. They died in a very tragic accident, the details of wish I do not want to share, but it was traumatic … the kind of thing a man doesn't get over easily, you understand. He fell into the bottle for a couple of years and finally came out of the grief a few months ago. I really thought he had come to accept it and move on…as best as one can anyway."

"This injury has obviously set him back. Such incidents can leave someone traumatized for life. But what about the other lady, Heidi?"

"Oh, she's just a lass… a little girl, eight years old. Tom had known her for only about six months, but she made quite an impression on him. He became a surrogate father to her. You see, her father died."

"Do you know of her whereabouts, Mr. Byrne?"

"I assume she is in the care of some orphanage in Cape Town."

"Such a tragedy." said the doctor, glancing at Tom through the glass.

"Well, if he were to see the child again, do you think it might make a difference…I mean, could he snap out of this?" inquired Weasel thoughtfully.

"I cannot state with certainty, but I have seen it work before. A visit from the past, something that jogs a memory or stimulates emotion, could help him recover."

"Well, that settles it, doctor. I need you to take good care of me, best friend, here while I go find a wee lass in the grand city of Cape Town. Wish me luck!" said Weasel with a grin as he slapped the doctor on the shoulder and, nearly danced his way down the hallway and disappeared down the stairs.

"Odd man that Byrne," murmured Gerhardt as he scribbled some notes on his clipboard and proceeded in the opposite direction.

Later that day, Gerhardt made a stop at Tom's room to check on him, only to find him sitting upright in his bed with clouds of grey smoke hovering above him. The sweet smell of tobacco that repulsed Weasel enveloped the sterile room in a blasphemous way. Tom smirked and inhaled deeply, letting out a ring of smoke in the doctor's general direction. He was quite proud of himself.

"It is such a delight to see you making such remarkable progress, Mr. Sutton," said Doctor Gerhardt with an air of sarcasm.

Tom plucked the cigar from his teeth and extended his hand towards the doctor, who kept his hands firmly on his clipboard.

"Thank you, doctor. Praise to the Lord, I say, whose bounties are fathomless."

"Well, if that's the case, perhaps we should stop Mr. Byrne. He does not need to board that train to Cape Town. Don't you agree, Mr. Sutton?"

Tom realized quickly that the doctor had unraveled his plan. "And this is a non-smoking hospital, Mr. Sutton, especially for a patient like you." said the doctor curtly as he relinquished Tom his cigar, tamping it out on the back of his clipboard.

"You can chase a horse, doctor, but not Timothy Byrne. He's probably already on a train to Cape Town by now." teased Tom as the doctor crossed the room to exit, slightly worried that he actually might try and stop him.

"I hope you do acknowledge that you have been deceitful under my care Mr. Sutton. And you have sent Mr. Byrne on a wild goose chase for your benefit when there clearly is no need. I hope you know what you're doing."

"I do acknowledge that, doctor. And are you not being paid generously by my kind boss for my care and my hospital stay, doctor?" said Tom in a slightly mocking tone.

"No more cigars!" said Gerhardt grabbing his cigar and confiscating it to the breast pocket of his white coat. "For your own good health Mr. Sutton! Oh, and I shall be prescribed a dose of castor oil twice a day to ensure that your delicate digestive system does not suffer due to constipation." He continued, "And because of your employer's generous compensation, we won't want to compromise on your hygiene either, Mr. Sutton, so I shall have Nurse Van der Berg personally assist you in a bed bath each morning for the duration of your stay with us." and with that Gerhardt closed the door behind him with a supercilious smirk.

"Wait! I take it all back, doctor. Wait, no…. not that Milch Frau!" Tom bellowed after him as he disappeared from his periphery.

CHAPTER 14

The Weasel's Lie

easel sat nervously, rolling the lining of his hat between his fingers over and over in his lap. The stark room with its pearl-white walls and ceiling reminded him of the hospital. Upon his arrival at the institution on Long Street, the arched entryway and cruciform layout had seemed oddly churchlike to him. The little white-haired gatekeeper had taken his name for the visitor's book upon entrance and then scurried off suspiciously.

The building had been in operation for some hundred years already, tied to the Groot Kirk Dutch Reformed Church in South Africa. Given his liaison to the church community, it made abundant sense that the Dutchman, Heidi's father, would have felt comfortable placing Heidi in their care. Weasel observed some children taking lessons and others chattering cheerfully in the hallways as he was ushered to the administrator's office. The orphanage seemed well run, and the children looked cared for here. His eyes came to rest on Mrs. Ingrid Koning, a broad-shouldered woman who kept a tight schedule and withstood no nonsense from her subjects. Koning was a fitting name for the orphanage's administrator, for she was the "king" of this institution and commanded her subjects accordingly. Weasel watched with trepidation as she examined Heidi's file through her spectacles while ushering messengers in and out of her office with clear instructions, usually in Afrikaans. He had never seen a woman wield authority so effortlessly. Her tight grey bun coiled upon her head was indicative of her sense of order and constraint. She wore a crisp, form-fitting black dress with a lace blouse that buttoned to her neck, fixed with a plain silver brooch. So far, she had barely given him any eye contact, merely peering over her glasses as he asked a myriad of questions about Heidi, to which she simply responded with an emotionless yes or no.

Obviously, his ingratiating Irish wit and charm were not disarming the "king", and Weasel contemplated his antics as he continued rolling the rim of his hat through his fingers nervously and decided to try a more somber approach. If he were to have Heidi accompanied him back to Johannesburg; he would have a better sound and be more convincing.

"Why didn't you and Mr. Sutton come to see Heidi earlier, Mr. Byrne? Her father died over six months ago." said the administrator without looking up.

"Well, you see, we had headed North…Northern Rhodesia, you know, madam," said Weasel sheepishly.

"I am aware of where Northern Rhodesia is," said Mrs. Koning sternly.

"Well, we were working on a modest farm when the news of little Heidi's loss came to us… …it took some time for the news to reach us." Weasel knew that dynamite and mines wouldn't fare well for his cause.

"I see. But her father never mentioned any Timothy Byrne." She said, flipping through Heidi's paperwork conscientiously.

"I can understand. Because I am not her real uncle, you see, unlike Thomas Sutton. But I am a good friend of Thomas'. As I said before, the reason I came in his place is that he has been involved in a terrible accident and is currently under treatment in Joburg. So, I came meself, for Heidi. He has been asking for her in his semi-conscious state, you see, and the doctors believe that seeing her in the flesh might help him recover."

Koning looked up momentarily and stared at him intensely, lowering her spectacles for the moment. "I am indeed sorry about

Mr. Sutton; may God grant him a quick recovery. But pardon me, Mr. Byrne, how do you propose I take your words to be true? I don't mean to be rude, but my ultimate responsibility is the welfare of the child, who has been left in our care."

"I can understand your concern, madam. But I have no reason to lie to you. You have the letter from Dr Gerhardt there explaining Tom…I mean her uncle's condition. If you don't believe me, ask little Heidi about me. And ask about her Uncle Tom and how much he loves her. You will find your confirmation there. I am also a practicing Catholic who attends mass every Sunday morning, religiously." The minute he uttered the words practicing Catholic, he knew that he had ruffled her feathers, and he wasn't sure if it had helped or hindered his plea.

Koning only nodded in affirmation and, through pursed lips, called out from her desk in Afrikaans. A young windswept young woman, who seemed a touch excitable, appeared at the door and, without acknowledging Weasel, came to the edge of Koning's desk.

"Ja Mevrou?" said the young woman, looking eager to please. "Margaretha, can you bring Heidi Van Wyk to my office? "Ja Mevrou," she said with a smile and abruptly exited.

"Care for some tea while we wait for Little Heidi?" said Koning rather pleasantly.

"Yes, please, madam," Weasel said, heaving a sigh of relief. He hadn't eaten since he left Johannesburg, and only at the suggestion of tea did he realize how famished he was. Besides, he had just passed the first obstacle, and so he relaxed, abandoning his hat in the chair next to him and moving to the settee and tea table next to her desk, where a formidable tea service was soon brought in at the "king's behest.

Across the road from the orphanage stood a modern Edwardian baroque building, which was all the rage in the new twentieth-century Johannesburg. Its majestic domed corner rooftop pavilions and large frontal ionic columns dwarfed the older buildings around it. Through the window of the orphanage, you could just about decipher the title *"Atkins & Wilkinson, Solicitors, and Commissioner of*

Oaths" etched elaborately on an iron plate positioned prominently on the front door.

In the front left office, Wilkinson sat behind his desk, with his back to the street below, interrogating the frail white-haired orphanage gatekeeper, who had arrived only moments before after a strenuous climb up the front steps of the monolith.

"You wanted to know if someone came to visit Little Heidi Van Wyk, sir."

"Yes. Go on," answered Wilkinson impatiently.

"Well, a man just arrived all the way from Johannesburg to visit Miss Van Wyk in the orphanage. Small and skinny chap. And…he's a paddy!"

Wilkinson stood suddenly and looked skeptically at the guard. He had waited six months for this day and had almost given up. Rounding the desk, he came face to face with the old man, who wasn't much shorter than he was.

"Are you certain that the man came to see Heidi Van Wyk?" "As certain as I can be."

"Did the Irishman leave a name behind?"

"He signed himself in as Mr. Byrne in my gate book."

While the name rang no bell in Wilkinson's memory, he rushed to a filing cabinet in the corner of the room and started rustling through documents roughly. His bulky fingers fumbled over the file folders until he pulled out the pale blue file labelled VAN WYK. The old man looked on nervously as Wilkinson returned to his desk and hastily began fingering through the contents of the file, licking his thumb, and flipping with agility over pages searching for "Byrne". He used his index finger to read through pieces of text and then suddenly stopped abruptly on a piece of writing."

"Yes! The only living friend of Thomas E. Sutton, a small, wiry Irishman named Timothy Byrne." Wilkinson said exuberantly, pulling out ten shillings from his trouser pocket and thrusting it into the wrinkled hand before him.

"You have finally proven yourself worthy, Jacob. Now, I'll be grateful to know when he leaves and where he is headed. Try to get his exact whereabouts if you can. And, if he ever returns with a larger Irishman as his companion, I'd be most delighted to know Jacob." At that, Jacob's eyes lit up in hopes of being granted more rewards for his due diligence as the orphanage gatekeeper.

Wilkinson's whole demeanor had changed. This time, he was far more pleasant as he escorted the old man out of his office and gently closed the door behind him. Sitting back at his desk, he took a cigarette from the ornate silver cigarette box sitting by the desk lamp and lit it. Leaning back in his chair, he smoothed the few remaining hairs that straddled his shiny bald head and inhaled. The solicitor closed his eyes momentarily, letting the worry wrinkles around his eyes relax. Thomas Sutton, or at least his associate, had finally attempted to make contact with young Heidi Van Wyk. He had begun to think this Mr. Sutton had been a ghost of his friend and client Van Wyk's imagination. He had been, after all, very sick when they last met to amend his will. This was an unusual case, to be sure, and a personal one for him. He wished no more than to honor his departed friend's request and see to it that his young daughter had the future she deserved.

Across the street, Weasel had been struggling through some polite conversation with the administrator while enjoying the malva pudding and strong hot tea. Before long, the busy young woman returned with Heidi. Koning rose and blocked Weasel from her view so she could aptly observe the reaction to their reunion.

"Heidi, I have a visitor for you."

"Who is it?" exclaimed Heidi as Koning stepped aside, revealing Weasel.

"Uncle Tim?" Heidi shouted with excited disbelief before nearly knocking over Koning and crashing into Weasel's open arms. He moved to the floor, and on his knees, he engulfed Heidi in a big hug as the administrator observed. Heidi's reaction couldn't have been more perfect. Once the reunion was over, all three settled themselves back around the tea table. Koning brought her notebook along and recorded her observations as they chatted effortlessly. Placing the pen aside, she looked up and offered Heidi a small smile.

"Heidi, my dear, so you obviously know this man. But please tell me how he is related to you?"

"Oh, Uncle Tim is my… uncle? she hesitated. "But Uncle Tom is my real uncle. Papa told me so." Heidi smiled enthusiastically.

"Aha," said Koning

"That's me best mate, Thomas Edward Sutton, madam. The man I told you about."

Heidi sensed the same discretion in his voice and familiar wink he used to employ when he and Tom had attempted to discuss "adult things" in her presence in the past. She couldn't be hoodwinked this time. "Did something happen, Uncle Tim? Is Uncle Tom alright?"

Weasel looked to Koning for permission and proceeded. "No, Heidi. Uncle Tom had an accident."

"He had an accident." uttered the child with a look of horror on her face.

"Well, you see, we were coming to see you". He lied. "But the big fancy automobiles you see around here, one hit him badly. He is in the hospital now. But he keeps calling out for you, lass."

Weasel wagered that a plea to the administrator in front of Heidi might help his cause. It was obvious that the child was well-liked here, and he was sure the Dutchman had paid the institution healthily before his death. Given his personal experience with the girl, Weasel knew that her spirit was infectious. She was indeed a delight and, to be sure, a fair manipulator herself.

"Madam, please let me bring the child to her uncle, just for a short period of time. As a God-fearing Irishman, I give you my word."

Heidi's round blue eyes filled with tears, and she simply looked at Mrs. Koning and said softly, "Madam, please. Let me go to my Uncle Tom. He is all the family I have. It must be God's will that he seeks me at this moment."

Weasel was impressed. While he knew Heidi's feelings for Tom to be true and altruistic, her manipulation of the God card was pure genius. The administrator had no choice but to honor God's wishes. As tears rolled freely down Heidi's rosy cheeks, the administrator reached for the child's hand, patted it comfortingly, and called out into the hallway. The same windswept young woman returned.

"Margarethe, please take Heidi to her room and help her pack her belongings for a one-week trip to Johannesburg. Grinning from ear to ear, the tears dried quickly. Heidi took Margarethe's hand with gusto and exited the administrator's office to pack her essentials. As soon as they were out of sight, Koning turned to face Weasel, who stood watching with a supercilious grin etched on his face. She smiled at him. Her approval could convert even the most robust of soldiers, thought Weasel.

"So, what part of Ireland are you from, Mr. Byrne?"

"I am a Dubliner…from Dublin," Weasel realized how stupid he sounded as soon as the words had escaped his lips.

"Very well then, Mr. Byrne. You understand this is highly irregular. Please sign this release document, which will be kept here on file and turned over to the City Court should it not be met." She pushed a document towards him titled "Temporary Release of Minor" I expect to see Miss Heidi Van Wyk back here in my office in precisely a week. And for future reference, if you wish to obtain custody of Heidi, I will need you to surrender an official verification that Mr. Sutton is indeed her relative."

"Yes, Madam!" Weasel said, looking up from the document and nodding in compliance. It hadn't really occurred to him that someone might wish to steal a child from such a place for nefarious reasons until this moment. He had only been thinking of Tom ailing in a hospital bed and the happiness Heidi would bring him by her mere presence.

He suddenly felt oddly exposed and surreptitious. He had, after all, fabricated the story and even lied about the accident and their whereabouts these past six months. What would stop a real deviant from doing the same, he wondered. But Heidi's affirmation had been the lynchpin, he thought decidedly. Without her affirmation, Koning would never have approved; at least, he had hoped so.

His mind swirled as he smiled awkwardly at the administrator and pretended to scour the paper before him. He was convinced that she could read his thoughts. He quickly finished skimming the document and signed the release, handing it boisterously to Koning and changing the subject.

"Madam, you seem to be intrigued with my place of origin. Have you ever been to Ireland?

"No! And no, I'm not intrigued, Mr. Byrne, simply curious. You see, I don't trust the Irish, and I am not sure I completely trust you, Mr. Byrne. If you are a God-fearing man, as you so say, I expect that you will honor our agreement!" Koning took the signed document from Weasel and carefully placed it in Heidi's document folder, closing the leather portfolio with a twist of the brass lock.

Without giving Weasel eye contact, she turned and placed the portfolio in the cabinet behind her. Pulling a set of assorted keys from her dress pocket, she instinctively found the small key and locked it with a click. Turning to face Weasel, she smiled pleasantly and took a sip of tea from the cold blue china cup that sat poised on the edge of her desk.

Heidi saved Weasel from any further scrutiny as she bounced back into the room with Margarethe trailing behind with her small suitcase and travelling coat. The administrator smiled at the little girl, called her to her desk, and reiterated the instructions to Heidi. The girl nodded cheerfully, unaware of what had transpired in her absence. Weasel quickly claimed Heidi's hand and, with the other, relieved Margarethe of Heidi's suitcase and coat. He gave Mrs. Koning the sincerest nod that he could muster, hoping that she would find some assurance in his Irish eyes that the child would be safe in his care. He thought he saw a glimpse of approval from the administrator as they rounded her office door and sped down the hallway into the city.

The two chattered away like two long-lost friends as they made their way to the station. Weasel purchased two tickets for the next departing train to Johannesburg and some licorice for them to share, and they settled down on the bench to wait for the train. Weasel listened empathetically as Heidi related the death of her father and how hard it was to endure it alone. Weasel felt guilty for having left when they did, although she blamed no one. Her young life had turned upside down quickly, and her future had no real direction, yet her demeanor remained unflinchingly positive.

He was grateful to know that the orphanage had not been a terrible life sentence and that Heidi had made friends and got into the good graces of the administrator and teachers alike. That did not surprise him. She was now brighter than ever, full of enthusiasm and wit. She knew how to ingratiate people, and she knew how to earn people's loyalty. She was a survivor.

Their chattering was abruptly interrupted by a diminutive, balding man who appeared before them, full of importance. "Mr. Byrne, young Heidi Van Wyk, I presume?"

Weasel placed an arm around the little girl's shoulder protectively. After all, he was now her guardian, and that made him feel quite important.

"Who the hell are you?" Weasel snapped as he rose quickly from the bench, causing Heidi to reprimand him for his impolite language. Both men disregarded her concern as the mysterious interloper proceeded to introduce himself.

"I go by the name of Theodore Wilkinson, esquire." He extended his hand to Weasel, who promptly ignored the gesture.

"And what do you want from me? I don't know you."

"Oh, but I know you, Mr. Byrne." said the solicitor, grinning.

"Will you get on with the bloody riddles and get to the point, man!" said Weasel with irritation.

"Uncle Tim! You are not being very careful with your language!" Heidi yelled at the grown man as she now stood and pointed her little finger at him sternly. Weasel bit dramatically at the air before him.

"And little girls should not be pointing fingers at their adults. It is bad manners. I'll bite that finger off if you keep waving it in my face." Heidi wasn't fazed by the threat and laughed.

"May I be so rude as to disrupt your reunion?" Wilkinson took their attention once more.

"Look, mate, get on with it. We have a train to catch," said Weasel with a wink to Heidi.

Wilkinson wasn't used to being spoken to with such hostility and irreverence. He snapped back in an authoritative tone. "Mr. Byrne; would you be kind enough to deliver the following message to Mr. Sutton? Charles. A. Van Wyk was my client and friend, and it was his final wish that Mr. Sutton would visit my office before he visited his daughter. When I was informed today of your arrival, I had hoped Mr. Sutton would be travelling with you. But since he was not, it is imperative that he receive this message should he accompany you on your return to Cape Town to deliver Miss Van Wyk to Children's Home. All I ask is that he honors the wishes of Miss Van Wyk's father. That is all. My office is located opposite the orphanage. The modern building with the columns. I'm sure even you can put that to memory."

Heidi's eyes had swelled with unwelcome tears at the mention of her father's name, and despite Weasel's pride being slightly dented by Wilkinson's insult, he was nonetheless intrigued by the request. Weasel pulled Heidi close and allowed her to unleash her sobs into his chest. He decided that whatever business this solicitor had with Tom, it must be legitimate and important, and turning to Wilkinson, he said earnestly, "You have my word," and shook his hand.

In an instant, the bald man had disappeared into the crowd that had assembled to board the train and was gone. Reaching into his pocket, Weasel retrieved his handkerchief and wiped Heidi's eyes. "Where is that brave little spirit I know? Let's go and see your Uncle Tom." Weasel clasped her hand tightly and gathered up her suitcase, and together, boarded the train to Johannesburg.

CHAPTER 15

The Reunion

Mostly for his own benefit, Weasel tried to keep the conversation with Heidi light and unrelated to the mission at hand. He didn't want his mind to keep sinking into dire images of his friend lying unconscious in a hospital bed, mumbling incoherently every time Heidi mentioned Tom's name. Weasel desperately needed his friend to recover.

They stepped off the train in Johannesburg and made their way to the hospital on foot. With fingers locked in a tight grip of anticipation, Heidi tried to keep up with Weasel's incessant pace. As they climbed the hospital's lobby steps, Heidi was deep in her own anxiety, brooding over the tragedies she had had to endure already in her short life. Losing both her parents had taken a toll on her young faith. She still believed in God and said her prayers every night like her father had taught her. But why had her Uncle Tom left her, she questioned. And, now that they were to be reunited, surely God would not be so unkind as to take him from her life as well.

She decided she would not let that happen, as she observed the worried look Weasel had worn the whole journey back as he had tried to distract her from talking about Uncle Tom. She knew how to care for someone ill, she thought. She had done this before. Determined to see her Uncle Tom fully recover, she vowed that she wouldn't eat or sleep for a moment and would pray to God every day and night for his mercy until he was better.

Both their nostrils were bombarded with the astringent smell of Dakin's fluid and iodine as they passed the surgery ward. Heidi pinched her nose as they made their way to Tom's hospital room, where he was convalescing. Then, they both heard a familiar voice shouting in short grunts of displeasure.

A few feet from Tom's hospital door, Weasel and Heidi stopped dead in their tracks and shared a look of bewilderment. Without a single moment of hesitation, Weasel busted through the door with Heidi close behind, only to find a disheveled, ornery Tom, resisting Nurse Van der Berg and her ominous tablespoon of castor oil, which she was attempting to thrust into his gaping mouth. Heidi wasted no time at all and leapt at Tom with exuberance.

"Uncle Tom!"

"Heidi! My child!" Tom bellowed, knocking the spoon from the nurse's hand and reaching out from his bed to embrace Heidi. Recognizing that she would not win this battle, a defeated Nurse Van Der Berg scowled and left the room, taking her castor oil with her.

"You're not sick," squealed Heidi in delight, hugging Tom. Tom peered over the girl's shoulder to see a faint flicker of betrayal in Weasel's eyes as he turned around and left the room without a word. Tom was sorry he had misled his friend, but he knew that Weasel would never have agreed to retrace their past and bring Heidi to him otherwise. He knew that Weasel's anger would subside quickly and that Heidi's mere presence would mend their bad feelings. She had an uncanny knack for bringing people together. For now, he decided he would only focus on the girl. Having her here with him was the best medicine he could ask for, and he reckoned that they had both waited long enough for this reunion.

Heidi, too, felt a sense of euphoria, knowing that the months of care and devotion she had planned for weren't necessary and that her Uncle Tom would live. This time, she thought, she wouldn't let him say goodbye. After their tearful reunion, Heidi hopped onto the foot of Tom's hospital bed, and they laughed their way into a familiar volley of jokes and stories, just like they had done in the boarding house.

Not wanting to make a show of himself in front of the child, Tom became the model patient. He willingly succumbed to the tasteless hospital meals, endured his daily bed baths, and accepted the twice-daily doses of castor oil administered by a vexed Nurse Van Der Berg without nary a complaint. Weasel would drop Heidi off in the morning, and she would spend the day with Tom, chattering about the wild adventures she dreamed of having someday, like in the stories she had read in books, with their heroes and heroines. She was so much like Sean, he thought, with her lust for adventure and her wild imagination.

The duo ate together, filled their time playing games and cards, and laughed freely as if they had not missed a beat. Even Nurse Van Der Berg and Doctor Gerhardt took a liking to Heidi and softened towards Tom because of the child. Only Weasel remained standoffish and distant, speaking only a few words, without eye contact, when dropping off and picking up Heidi.

Weasel felt used and manipulated, and Tom knew it. Tom tried to initiate a conversation each time Weasel was present but was only supplied with one-word answers. Tom knew that an explanation and apology were long overdue, but he could not broach them in front of Heidi. He didn't want the child to come between them through no fault of her own. He had hoped that Weasel's anger would subside, and he would come to realize, as he had, how much they all needed each other. She deserved more than a future at an orphanage.

Tom compartmentalized his dispute with Weasel for the time being. He had so little time with Heidi and wanted to enjoy it before she had to return to Cape Town. On Heidi's second to last day, Weasel arrived, as usual, to pick her up but stopped short outside Tom's room to observe the two inconspicuously. Heidi was in tears, sitting at the end of his bed. Weasel leaned in closer to hear what she was saying.

"Uncle Tom, there is this little girl at the orphanage. Her name is Emily. Oh, I just love her Uncle Tom-she's so sweet. She has black hair and the bluest eyes, just like the ocean! Her parents died when they were coming back to fetch her from her auntie's house. She says their boat turned over. Then, she had to live with her auntie. And oh, what a mean woman she was. After her parent's death, she made Emily do all the chores, just like Cinderella, you know. She even washed their clothes at night and had to take care of her three little cousins. Emily said that all they did was cry and scream all the time. One time, she broke a plate when she was washing the dishes, and her auntie beat her black and blue and made her sleep on the verandah without dinner, so she ran away."

"Dear Lord, then how did Emily come to the orphanage, Heidi?"

"She was found on the side of the road by some people who were kind enough. She had walked very far, and she wasn't well. They took her to the hospital. After she got better, the hospital sent her to the orphanage. She told the orphanage that she had no family and made up a new name," She whispered, "So I don't think her real name is Emily. And her auntie never came looking for her."

"How old is she?"

"Oh, she is only a year older than me, Uncle Tom. She is just nine." Tom dabbed the tears on her cheeks with a handkerchief.

"So, do they care for you at the orphanage, Heidi? They won't hurt you there…or Emily, do they?" inquired Tom nervously.

"Oh no. They are quite nice at the orphanage. Very strict but fair. They don't beat any of us." said Heidi emphatically.

"Well, that's good to hear," said Tom relieved.

"But they don't really love us, Uncle Tom. They go home to their own children. I have what I need to live, but…it's not like having a mother or father to love and embrace you…or an uncle." she smiled sadly.

Tom realized that she wasn't plying her case this time but merely stating the objective truth about her new life. She wasn't manipulating him. Had she somehow lost that ability to wrap people around her finger, or had the orphanage driven it out of her? He couldn't imagine there was any room there for self-advocacy or favoritism.

Weasel also felt the weight of Heidi's words as he listened on the other side of the door. He reminded himself that he had had a mother and father and his dear brother Shamus as a boy. Life all alone without a family had to be very hard for a child. Then he thought of Tom, who had grown up in an orphanage, one that he was sure had lacked any real love and care and had been full of beatings. Tom never even liked talking about it. He couldn't imagine any child like Heidi being subjected to such a scarred childhood simply because of circumstances that were no fault of their own.

Peeking through the small window into the room, Weasel watched Tom take Heidi by both hands and say, "Little Heidi, you deserve a family. You deserve care and love and a home filled with joy. I only wish I could give that to you."

Weasel couldn't stop the tears that followed, and his anger for his friend dissipated. How could they let the orphanage determine Heidi's fate? Heidi had saved Tom many months ago, and now they had to do something to make her life more fulfilling. But what and how? He knew that Tom could not prove any familial link to Heidi by blood. He could not adopt her even if he wanted to as a single man, and besides, he did have his apprehensions about Tom raising a child given their current circumstances and employment.

Straightening his posture, Weasel cleared his throat to announce his arrival and entered the room.

"Uncle Tim! You are here!" said Heidi, bouncing off the bed and into his outreached arms.

"Why are your eyes red?" said Heidi, looking up at him as Weasel threw a glance at Tom and wiped his eyes with the back of his sleeve.

"Oh, from the dust. You know how the automobiles are driving by, stirring dust into the air."

Tom and Weasel exchanged a knowing look, and Tom knew that all was forgiven. Weasel smiled at Tom, who looked like he was in fine health, save for the sling. It was obvious that Heidi was good for him, and he needed her just as much as she needed him. Walking to his bedside, he slapped him playfully on the back, indicating that he no longer harbored any grudge. "About time you recovered, you dumb-arse," he said cheerily.

"Uncle Tim! Language! Also, you cannot hit Uncle Tom. He is still sick!" said Heidi, rushing to Tom's other side, protectively wagging her finger at him.

"What did I tell you about pointing the finger at an adult, little Heidi? Do you want me to bite your finger off?" Weasel teased as he snapped his teeth.

Tom looked to his right and to his left. Everything he cared about in the world right now was here by his bedside. He was the happiest he had been in years and didn't want this composition to change. He had to find a way to keep Heidi and her in his life.

"I am sorry, Weasel, for giving you a scare."

"A scare! You friggin wanker? You almost gave me a heart attack. If you missed the colleen so much, you could have just asked me. You know I would do anything for you, Sutton! I thought you were going to bloody die or, worse, go insane in the head." They both laughed as Heidi looked on with mock disapproval.

"Weasel, I'll have you know that I cannot be prouder of your running skills. I'm sure they came in handy, eh?"

"You have no idea! You had me running around like a bloody jack-arse. And talking to that Mrs. Koning at the orphanage was no picnic either, I'll have you know. Weasel shivered in mock fear.

"Uncle Tim, if you don't mind, at least wait until tomorrow when I'm not around anymore… to use your wild language." They all laughed until their sides hurt.

With Heidi's departure looming closer, Weasel had to agree that now that the connection had been recovered, they could not sever it again. Not caring that Heidi was present, Weasel spoke candidly.

"My dear friend… Heidi here is the key to keeping you two connected. Now, the orphanage will not concede to any type of ongoing relationship unless you provide legal verification that you're Heidi's blood relative, which we all know you can't."

"But Papa said you were as good as my real Uncle, didn't he, Uncle Tom?" said Heidi emphatically

"I know, lass, but this time, they only let you come because of the letter from Dr Gerhardt about your Uncle Tom's condition." Weasel smiled slyly, recognizing how brilliant Tom's ruse had really been.

"What do you mean, Uncle Tim?"

"What Uncle Tim means is that it is only because I was sick that they let you come. Without the papers showing that I'm your real uncle, they won't let you come again or let me visit you at the orphanage," said Tom, explaining.

"So, you see, child, without any official papers, it's up to you to convince Mrs. Koning that Uncle Tom is your real uncle. You will have to explain that we drifted apart over the years but that we are back now and want to be able to be a part of your life. "Can you do that, Heidi?"

"Oh, yes, Uncle Tim. I know what to do." beamed Heidi.

"I always want to be in your life, Heidi. So, while you work on Mrs. Koning, I'll learn everything I can about farming and Northern Rhodesia." Tom assured her.

That night, all three of them slept in the same hospital room. Heidi cuddled into Tom's good arm while Weasel sprawled out on the guest couch tucked in the corner. Dawn came too soon for Tom as the little creature, whom he had come to love as his own, gathered up her belongings and bid him a final farewell. Her deep emotional eyes were expectedly watery as she clung to Tom's neck, unwilling to relinquish the human touch that she had been denied these many months. Tom didn't want to let go either. In the depths of his soul, he wanted to protect this little girl, care for her, and provide for her. She wanted to be her father. Weasel carefully pried the two apart, reminding them gently of the train's departure.

"Come on now. This isn't goodbye. Just a farewell for now, alright." said Weasel sympathetically.

"I'll come and see you soon, Heidi. When I leave the hospital. I promise." said Tom, gripping her little hands tightly and looking deep into her eyes, hoping that she took him for his word.

Weasel took Heidi by the hand as she let go of Tom's and scooped up her small suitcase.

"Come, lass, I don't want to miss the train."

"Yes, Uncle Tim," Heidi said seriously, taking the task at hand with the utmost priority. "We will be together soon, Uncle Tom… promise!" Heidi crossed her fingers and waved them at Tom, who returned the gesture with a nod, and they set off for the train station.

TO BE CONTINUED......

Book Two
THE DUTCHMAN'S PLAN

www.ingramcontent.com/pod-product-compliance
Lightning Source LLC
Chambersburg PA
CBHW031048310726
48969CB00007B/2179